MILLSTONE

Colin Neville

How can life bring you to such a dark place so quickly?

It would be better for him to be thrown into the sea with a millstone tied around his neck than for him to cause one of these little ones to sin (Luke 17.2).

January: The Feast of St. Agnes

Jayne Boyle walked along the school corridor. It was morning break and the children were in the playground. But in one classroom she saw Tracy Banks drawing on the whiteboard. Two other nine year old girls, Latesha and Millie, looked on, giggling. She went in.

'What are you girls doing in here?'

They turned with shock toward her.

'What have you been drawing on the board, Tracy?'

She had drawn a picture of a male figure with an erect penis. The man was stretching out his hands and was holding a smaller figure; their heads were touching.

Jayne Boyle stared in horror at the drawing, 'What's this?'

Tracy started to cry. Jayne ignored this. 'Explain! Now! '

Tracy shook her head.

'Who's the man supposed to be? And who is this?' Jayne pointed at the other figure.

Tracy looked in dumb horror at the Deputy Head Teacher. Jayne bent down and took her by the shoulders. 'Tell me, girl!'

‘It’s Mr. Young.’

‘Mr. Young!’

Tracy nodded. Jayne recovered her composure. ‘And who is this?’ She pointed at the other figure.

‘It’s me.’

‘You! And what is…Mr. Young supposed to be doing?’

‘He’s kissing me.’

Jayne said quietly, ‘Are you making this up? This is a very, *very* serious thing indeed to say about a teacher.’

Tracy shook her head. ‘No, he loves me; he loves me. And he kissed me!’

Chapter One

One month earlier

December: The Feast of St. Nicholas

The low wall around the school playground was topped with a six foot wire fence. From the outside, the scene resembled a giant cage containing some troublesome group of primates that ran, pushed, clustered, and orbited around each other.

Bryan Young coasted into the playground on his bike, a yellow plastic helmet skewed on his head, like some carbuncled banana. The children gathered round. 'You look like 'The Predator,' Mr Young.'
He exterminated them with his ray gun fingers and the boys fell, suitably zapped.
'I wish these were real, I'd have you lot under control in no time. The other teachers would be queuing up for one; I'd make a fortune.'
'Sir…knock, knock!'
'O, here we go! Who's there?'
'Lucy.'
Bryan had heard it before. 'Lucy who?'
'Luc-elastic makes your pants fall down!'

All the children laughed. One imitated a drummer: '…Pants fall down; see your bum, bum, bum.'
A hulking older boy, Wayne, pushed his luck: 'Why do women rub their eyes in the morning?'
Bryan shook his head. 'Don't know.'
'They don't have balls to scratch!'
Bryan tried not to laugh, and he could see some of the younger children were thinking about this. 'Alright… that's enough entertainment for one day. We're going to blow your minds with loads of lovely learning today.' The children groaned.
Bryan remembered a riddle. 'What would you get if you crossed a vampire and a teacher?' They didn't know.
'Lots of blood tests!' More groans. The children drifted away, the drummer still drumming: 'Bum bum, bum.'

Bryan secured his bike and entered the school. He was in his thirties, casually dressed in jeans, and loose fitting shirt; there was a shadow of stubble on his face.
The school was decorated for Christmas, and the classrooms were bright with coloured streamers, baubles, and festive drawings. In reception the 'Welcome to Our School' sign was hung with silver and gold tinsel. There was a wooden and straw-topped nativity tableau nearby, with white and blue linen tacked down to the floor around the crib. Mary and Joseph, plus a handful of other plaster figures, knelt over

a baby, remarkably large for its newly-born age, and already extending its arms to the world.
Christine, another teacher his own age, greeted him and they stopped at the crib.
Bryan splayed out his arms. 'Look, he wants his gold, frankincense and myrrh…gimmee, gimmee!'
Christine laughed, 'He'd fit in alright round here then! But don't let 'HMV' hear you utter such blasphemy.'

As if on cue, 'HMV,' or Jayne Boyle, the Deputy Head, came out of the general office. She was in her late fifties, dressed plainly in white blouse, fawn cardigan and tweed skirt. Her greying hair was swept back into a tight bun at the back of her head. She wore no jewellery, but a gold crucifix was attached to her blouse, and a pair of bi-focal glasses swung around her bosom on a chain. She had given up the fight to control her weight.
'Good to see you so happy on a Monday morning,' she trilled, as if addressing her class.
'Well, we're always happy to be here, Jayne,' Bryan said, affecting a 'thousands wouldn't believe me' tone.
'I don't want to spoil things for you,' Jayne said, in similar vein, 'but I would be glad if you would cover the playground today; Mary's phoned in sick.' She stopped herself with an effort from saying, 'again.'

Bryan thought of other staff members she could have asked, but decided to hold this back. He knew why she had asked him. She took his silence as acquiescence.
'Well, that's good then. *Don't run!*''
The boy skidded into a jerky walk and glanced nervously at her.

'I think she's still peeved about your salary,' said Christine as she and Bryan collected their mail from the office. 'Joan in the office told me that it puts you above her now. She must know this herself by now. If Joan hasn't told her, the Head would have done!'
'I can't help that. I brought the grade with me from the other school.'
Before Bryan had left his last school he had applied for and eventually been designated an 'Advanced Skills Teacher,' for his work on teaching English, with an increase in salary that now took him into a senior level.
A bell sounded in the corridor and they made their way to morning assembly. Children suddenly appeared, jostling from all directions.

The hall, which doubled as the school dining area, still retained the odour of minced beef, custard, and pasta from Friday's lunch. The children, aged from five to ten, swarmed in noisily and sat down facing the stage. The teachers followed and lined the sides. Miss Cottrell got into position at the piano. Thomas Wood, the Head, Jayne Boyle, and Father Kelly, the school priest, sat at the front of the stage; Jayne looked steadily up at Thomas as he stood.

Thomas looked out at the children over the top of his half-moon glasses and waited until all was quiet. He was a serious-looking man in his late forties, dressed in a tweed blazer, grey trousers, white shirt and plain brown tie.

'Good morning, children.'

'Good-morning-Mister-Wood,' the children piped back.

'We'll begin with a prayer. Stand up, please. Father Kelly will lead us.'

Father Kelly arose with an effort. As his bulk settled, he joined his hands solemnly in prayer and said carefully, as if all present were slow-witted, 'Good morning children.'

'Good-morning-Father-Kelly.'

'We'll say the Lord's Prayer… In the name of the Father, the Son, and….'

'…the holy ferret,' whispered one boy in the third row, mimicking the priest's accent, and audible enough to be heard by the children in front. There was a subdued titter.

Father Kelly glowered in that direction, '…the Holy Spirit.'

The children crossed themselves. Those being coached for their first communion, made elaborate and slow gestures, whilst the more seasoned looked as if they were whisking troublesome flies from their face and chest.

'Our Father who art in heaven…'
The children picked up the chorus, '…and forgive those that trespass against us…and lead us not into temptation. *Amen.*'
Thomas nodded at Miss Cottrell, who began to pick out the opening chords of 'All things Bright and Beautiful.' Her voiced shrilled, slightly out of tune on the higher notes: 'All things bright and *beautiful….'*
The children followed, knowing the words after hearing them so often in Assembly.

Thomas read out a few announcements. He had introduced a House system, with good points awarded to children for their special efforts and good behaviour. There was a weekly House winner, announced at the start of each week.
'Luke House was the winner last week, and I understand that Joan Greenwood has won the House prize for a poem she has written. Where are you, Joan?' Joan rose shyly. 'Please come to the front, Joan, and read your poem.'
Doing as she was bid, she read it, almost in one breath:
'There's-litter-all-around-us-there's-litter-on-the-street-there's-litter-in-the bushes-there's-litter-at-your-feet.'
She paused for the final effect: 'To drop your litter on the street really is a sin. So-please-be-kind-to-all-of-us-and-put-it-in-the-bin.'
Thomas beamed. This was a topic that recurred at Assembly.

‘Well done, Joan. An important subject - and one I have often spoken about.’ There was a chill to his words.
Joan bounced back to her place.
Bryan thought he had seen the poem before somewhere, probably on the Internet. He wondered about cheating and if plagiarism was a sin, too.

Chapter Two

The junior school, The Holy Apostles, was wedged into a rectangle of land between two main roads both leading to the main shopping area for the district, an eastern suburb of London. The two-storeyed building, built in the 1930s, stood, solid and grey, surrounded by a concrete playground, and next to the local Catholic Church that gave its name to the school.

Bryan's classroom was on the ground floor. It was a large square room, walls painted in yellow, with windows to one side overlooking the playground. Eight wooden tables in bright colours and assorted plastic chairs were spread out around the room. Ranged along the walls were shelves lined with books, the children's art and marked project work, posters, and examples of the rules of English and Mathematics. One colourful poster had the caption 'Class Rules,' with appeals to 'Listen,' 'Concentrate on Your Work,' 'Follow Directions,' and 'Respect Others.' Low cupboards were labelled 'Paper,' 'Pens,' and one group of cupboards had individual drawers for each child, labelled with their names. Christmas steamers had been strung along the tops of the walls in waves of red, green, silver and blue.

At the front of the room, high on a wall, was a framed picture of a doleful Jesus, his finger pressed to a blazing heart, and in the corner of the room, the children had built their own nativity scene from cardboard boxes, complete with paper-mâché figures. Around it, stuck to the wall, a work in progress, were the children's group drawings representing each stage of the Advent Story. Bryan had slipped away from assembly to arrive before the children and had written the lesson plan for the morning on the whiteboard: 'Vocabulary: Using the Right Word.' He had written four columns headed respectively 'Like'; 'Dislike'; 'Hate'; and 'Love.'

The children arrived. Bryan greeted them with a nod or word for a particular child and they filed in and went to the tables. Tracy Banks took hold of his hand, and swung on it, 'Hello Mr. Young.'
'Hi Tracy, nice to see you, are you OK today?'
She nodded, and ran to her place and began whispering to the other girls on her table.
They were a mixed group of nine year olds, with roughly equal numbers of boys and girls.
'Mobile phones?' A few children handed them in. They chattered together easily. Bryan knocked on his desk.
'Knock, knock.'

The children, used to his ways, chanted in unison, 'Who's there?'
'Ivor.'
The children hadn't heard this one. 'Ivor who?' they yelled.
'I've a good idea for our English lesson today!'
The children chorused 'awww', but were curious.
'I was in the playground last week and I heard one girl say to another, "I *hate* you!" '
He acted out the pouting and hands on hips scenario he had witnessed. The children laughed.
'OK. Let's think about words that we use. Look at the words on the board. There's 'like' and 'love,' and there's 'hate' and 'dislike.' But what do these words really mean?'
The children listened, interested.
He organized the distribution of writing paper, dictionaries and pens and asked them to work in groups
He moved around the room supervising their work.
'What's the difference between 'like' and 'love? Let's start with Red Group.'
Hands went up on the table. 'Tommy.'
Tommy said, 'like' is when you… like something…but not as much as love.'
'OK, give us an example.' Tommy thought for a minute. 'I like watching the telly, but I …I love my dog.'
'Good…so love is a much stronger feeling, would you say?'
Tommy nodded.

'Very good. Now let's look at 'hate.' Look it up. Everyone, please; you too, Charlie.'
The children thumbed through their dictionaries. Kate and Lucy found it together.
'It means to de…test something or someone…a powerful feeling of de…test…tation…very strong emo..tion.'
'Good. So to hate is when you have very strong, bad, bitter feelings that last a long time about someone or something.'
The children nodded.
The children then looked up 'dislike.'
Bryan said 'So 'dislike' is the opposite of 'like.' So if you have a quarrel with someone in the playground that you normally get on OK with, do you 'hate' them – or 'dislike' them for a while? Rose, what do you think?'
Rose considered. Bryan had heard her use 'hate' about another girl in the class.
'Dislike is better, I suppose, unless I really *hated* that person!'
I *hate* eating rice,' volunteered a boy, Peter.
'Well, I'm not keen on it either,' said Bryan. 'But is it really about *hating* it, or just disliking it? I don't have bad and bitter feelings about eating rice, but I wouldn't go out of my way to eat it if I had a choice. So maybe dislike is a better word to use. What do you think, Peter?'
'I still hate it!' said Peter.

Bryan asked them to work on their own and write sentences using each word. He gave examples about himself first. He wrote and repeated:
'I dislike being stuck in traffic jams on motorways.'
'I hate to see animals treated cruelly.'
'I love my mum and dad.' His parents were dead, but he still felt love for them. He was going to write 'Jennifer and Adam,' but decided against this, as it would take a personal explanation he thought better not to share with the class. 'I like riding my bike.'

They began to slowly write their own sentences and Bryan circled round the class. He stopped beside a shy boy, Tom, who was struggling with the exercise, getting increasingly agitated. Bryan stooped down beside him. Tom was having problems separating out 'dislike' from 'hate,' and Bryan went over it again with him.
Tracy Banks came up to him, 'Sir! Sir!'
He turned away from Tom, irritated about the interruption, but kept in physical contact with him, his hand resting lightly on the boy's shoulder. He listened patiently to Tracy and answered her question, but it was something that, as usual, could have waited until he reached her table.

As Bryan moved around the class he noticed Latesha passing a note to Millie. He moved in quickly, 'You know

the rule about note passing in class. Let me see it, Millie, please.'
Millie flushed and passed the note to him. It had a crude drawing of a girl with 'Maureen Briggs, ugly, stinks, hate, hate' scrawled across it. Maureen was a girl on their table. She was a plain child, slow-thinking and withdrawn from the other girls, who steered away from her at break-times. She was on the verge of tears, and Bryan's temper rose.
'Come with me you two.' He went into the corner of the room with Latesha and Millie, shepherding them lightly with his hands. He fought to keep the temper out of his voice.
'I want an explanation from you two – now – about this. Tell me why you are doing this to Maureen?'
The two girls looked down at their shoes, neither spoke.
Bryan went for the more easily-led of the two: 'Millie?'
Millie looked quickly at Latesha, and dropped her eyes.
'Latesha. I have spoken to you before about this behaviour. It's bullying. Do you really want me to talk to your mother?'

The procedure, laid down by the head in cases like this, was to refer children to him. But Bryan preferred to deal with incidents himself by talking to parents when they collected their children, or even by visiting them at home, if necessary, although this was contrary to school guidelines. He lived in the district and was prepared to do it. The alternative was to risk a child being labelled by the Head, and other teachers, as 'difficult,' when often all it took was a word by the class teacher with the parents.

His appeal to the parents was that their child's behaviour was affecting, not just their own future, but the learning of their neighbour's children - and this was just plain selfish. The parent's reactions were often to defend their children in the face of all criticism, but they would usually agree, reluctantly, on the justice of this argument.
Many of the parents had suffered themselves at school from the disruption caused by the kids around them, made worse by the inability of a weak or defeated teacher to deal with the problem. They also liked his direct speech, delivered without superiority, and in a local accent.

'So why are you doing this?'
Latesha looked at Millie and giggled. She feigned indifference and looked away.
His temper got the better of him and he took hold of her arms. 'Look at me when I speak to you, Latesha!' He struggled to contain his dislike of her. She glared back at him defiantly.
'You are making it hard for me, Latesha. You know I will have to speak to your mother now.'
'I don't care'.

Bryan collected the children's writing and they changed activity. They were working on their group nativity paintings when the Head and Father Kelly arrived, nodded curtly to him, and gravitated to the crib. They stood in silence looking at it.

'Mary and Joseph…and the baby Jesus…with brown faces…strictly true, I suppose, if we take a realistic, historical perspective', said Father Kelly. Thomas said nothing.

They wandered round looking at the children's work. They stopped next to a group of boys. Their painting showed a heavily pregnant Mary next to a miniature Joseph, who stood apart from her, holding a donkey twice his size.

The priest said, 'Why have you painted Joseph smaller than the donkey – and Mary?'

When they didn't reply, Thomas said sharply, 'Answer Father Kelly. You are being spoken to. Charlie?'

'Cos he was a wimp,' said Charlie.

Father Kelly and Thomas were dumbfounded. Father Kelly recovered. 'A wimp'! Why on earth do you think that?'

'Well, he weren't the father was he?' said Charlie. 'Darren said he would have given her a right-hander if she'd did it to him,' continued Charlie, emboldened by the giggles of the other two boys.

‘And who is Darren?’ said Thomas. Mum’s latest bed companion, he thought.
‘Darren’s me brother.’
‘Your brother! This is a sinful thing for any Catholic to say,’ said Father Kelly.
‘He’s me step-brother,’ said Charlie, ‘…and he ain’t a Catholic!’

Bryan sighed. It was just his luck the Head and Father Kelly had picked on this table. Charlie was just repeating something he had heard at home. Parents in the area could believe in God and feel a sense of spirituality, particularly at weddings, baptisms, and funerals, but could still make jokes, or half-jokes, about their own religion. He felt this was generally a good thing: that the church no longer had them in its thrall. The recent sexual allegations involving priests and children in their care had also shaken their respect for the clergy. A priest did not automatically command their trust these days, just because he gave them communion or heard their confessions.

Father Kelly decided to make a point to the whole class. ‘Children! Your attention, please. I want to talk about Joseph, the husband of the Blessed Mary, Mother of God. Now this is a special time – a *holy time*. Christmas.

Christ-mass. It is when we celebrate the birth of Our Lord. Our Redeemer.'

He sensed the children drifting away from him; their eyes were unfocused glassily in his direction. He became more urgent than he knew he should be.

'Mary was visited by The Holy Spirit and she conceived…she was given the baby Jesus by God… for *us*! Now Joseph was a good man…a patient and good man… and he stood by Mary. *He stood by her!* Now that's real *goodness*, children. And that's more than I could say about some…'

He stopped, and regained his composure. 'Now, let us thank Mary for giving birth to the Lord Jesus, with Joseph beside her. Hail Mary, full of grace, the Lord is with thee…' The children followed the prayer.

Thomas indicated to Bryan to follow him into the school corridor. 'Do you ever challenge these attitudes, Bryan?'

Bryan felt his hackles rising. 'The older children find the whole business of the Virgin Birth difficult. It's the butt of jokes locally and…'

'Yes, jokes! That says it all. This school is about embedding *faith* in the lives of these children. And I think it is our job – in a *faith school* - to challenge ignorance and crude jokes like this, don't you? Challenge it, not condone it!'

Bryan felt his dislike of the man coming again to the surface. 'I don't condone it. If this sort of remark comes up in class, I talk to the children about it. I ask them where they heard these remarks. I ask them what they think about them, I ask them…'

'What they *think* about them! They are only nine, for heaven's sake! How can they know what they *think* about them? Our job is to teach them; to give them a moral explanation.'

Bryan shook his head impatiently. 'The children *do* think about these issues! A number of them, like Charlie, are in step-families, or know a family where a man is not the natural father to the children in the house. They do have ideas about how well, or not, a man can look after someone else's kids!'

The children pretended to be absorbed in their work, but were silently observing the two men through the glass panel of the door - and straining to hear what they were obviously arguing about.

'Yes! Step-families! More the pity in a Catholic school… and why is Mary depicted by that boy in such a gross way? Did you not think about reminding him he was painting the Mother of God, not some tart from Bennett's Castle Lane!'

'Mary was pregnant. That's what a pregnant woman can look like! The children live in a real world and look around them, and see real woman, their mums, sisters, aunties, pregnant, with real, big, swollen bellies!'

'There's too much reality for these children; too early for them in life. What about you, Bryan, helping them retain their childhood, their…their sense of innocence – as well as some respect for their faith?'

When the Head and Father Kelly had left the children were subdued. Charlie said, 'what was wrong with our picture?'

'Nothing! Don't worry.'

Chapter Three

At break the children spilled out to the playground. Bryan stopped Maureen. 'Are you alright?'
Maureen's eyes had welled with tears. She wore the school uniform, but her clothes were shabby and unpressed, her shoes scuffed. Her hair was lank, and there was a strong whiff of body odour from her.
'They don't like me! Nobody wants to play with me.' She wept, the tears rolling in grey lines down her face.
Bryan crouched beside her, and put his arm around her. He held her until she stopped crying. 'Come on, let's find Alice. She's a nice girl, and I know she likes you.'
He knew no such thing, but was certain Alice would be kind to her. Maureen's tears gradually dried and she brightened. Bryan walked her round the playground, holding her hand, giving her his full attention, chatting to her, as he knew the children would see and notice. Alice was playing ball with her friend, Tanya, but without fuss they both quickly included Maureen into their game.

Bryan joined Helen, a school teaching assistant, and they walked the circuit of the playground. The grey bleakness was lightened in places with games squares and circles painted on the concrete. There were tables and benches scattered around, and on one side there was a wooden gazebo, with benches for the children. Children hung out of its open windows and huddled along the benches, chattering easily to each other. Others milled around. One boy ran past, his arms extended like a plane, followed by another, both spitting bullets. Girls ran together, or huddled in groups, some walked in pairs or small groups, arms draped around each other. A few solitary children ran after the others, or hovered on the edges of groups, hoping to be noticed and included.

Helen was popular with the children. She was of unconventional appearance, with red hair in spikes like the Statue of Liberty crown and a combination of vivid orange and jet black clothes that made her stand out anywhere. She also had a presence. She walked with an easy, flowing grace, and in class she smiled and laughed her way out of most difficult situations with the children, who liked her, and wanted her to like them. This kept them in line, and when she spoke to them, they listened and vied for her attention and approval.

A group of boys approached her. 'Miss! Miss! Have you got a boyfriend yet?'
She shook her head. 'I can't find anyone as handsome as you, Ronnie!' she said.

The boys laughed and shoved Ronnie, who blushed to the tips of his curly red hair.
'Will you marry me, Miss?' said another boy, Wayne. 'We'll have lots of babies!' This set the boys off again, pushing at each other.
'Well, I don't know about the babies!' said Helen. 'I wouldn't mind a big house, though. Would you look after me, Wayne?'
'Yeah! I'll see you alright, Miss,' said Wayne. More laughter.
'Can I take your picture, Miss'? Charlie had a mobile camera-phone.
Bryan said, 'Charlie, you know the rule about phones.'
'Don't tell, Sir. I don't flash it around in class.'
Ronnie said, 'Good job. It's only titchy!' The boys howled in glee.
They gathered round Helen and she crouched down in their midst, her arms hugging them all in a squealing embrace. Charlie took his picture.
Groups of girls now came round attracted by the laughter.
'Can we have a picture with you, Sir?'
Bryan protested.
'O, go on, *please* Sir!
'No! Save your pictures for someone else. And you all know the rule about phones!'

‘Sir, Sir, come on, Sir. We love you!’ The girls pulled at him.

‘Alright. Come on, quickly then.’ He crouched down, and the girls fell over and around him in a tumbling heap. Tracy Banks had got him around the neck. Someone used their camera phone. ‘I love you,’ crooned Tracy, ‘love, love, love you.’

Bryan pulled away, but Tracy clung on. ‘Don’t be silly – and don’t forget our lesson, Tracy. About love, and liking,’ said Bryan.

‘I love, love, love you-ooo. I do-ooo.’ Tracy ran off.

Chapter Four

Bryan sat in the staff room and read the children's work. "I love my mum". "I hate going to bed when it is still light". "I dislike my sister sometimes". Latesha had written "I hate people who laugh at me", and "I love my dad". Tracy had written, "I hate Mrs Yates", a member of the school staff. And, "I love Mr. Young".

He was joined by Jayne Boyle. She wanted to know what was going on in the playground.

'Did I see one of the children using a camera phone?' There was a clear note of criticism in her voice.

He felt himself go on the defensive. 'It's hard to police this. I know it's school policy to try and keep them out of school, or hand them in at the start of the day, but I take the view that as long as they are kept out of class, that's the best we can do. We've tried appealing to the parents, and that doesn't work.'

'They can be a tool for bullying, as well as an opportunity for well-off children to flaunt their parent's money. We need to enforce this policy, Bryan.'

He could see the logic of this, but something about her, and the way she spoke, stirred him with echoes from the past.

'Rules are rules, eh Jayne? Must stick to the rules, come what may!'

She filed this comment away, along with his attitude, for another day. She was tempted to add that Advanced Skills Teachers needed to show a good example, but decided this might unearth an emotion buried elsewhere. She had made her point, and saw that it had hit home.

She noticed the children's work, and saw the words 'love' and 'hate.' She asked about the class, and he explained.

'Can I see their work?' He passed over the sheets, but he felt uneasy. She glanced through the work. 'Don't you think this is too advanced for this age group?'

The retort: 'If I did, I wouldn't have asked them to do it' came quickly to his mind, but he kept this back, although he did have doubts now about the whole exercise. But he was not going to admit it to her.

'Some did struggle to separate out the differences, particularly about love and hate. But they use these words too easily, particularly hate, and especially about other people in the class - so I wanted them to start thinking about what the words mean – and the impact of them.'

She had read Tracy's work, which was close to the top of the pile.

'Do you think it wise to encourage children to express their 'hate,' indeed – or 'love'- about members of staff?'

'I did not *encourage* any such thing! I think you are missing the point of the lesson.'

‘No. I am not missing the point. But I am not sure you quite appreciate it. Do you intend to talk to Tracy about this?’
She noted, with quiet pleasure, that his face betrayed his emotion, which was uncertainty.
When he did not reply, she pressed him, ‘I think you should, Bryan. I think the Head would agree with me: that you can open a Pandora’s Box if you are not careful. Some things are best contained.’ With that, and before he could think of a reply, she moved away from him to take up a more prominent position in the room for the staff meeting.

The other teachers and support assistants began to arrive. One had brought in a birthday cake and began to slice it for her colleagues; she gave these out as they arrived. The teachers began to take familiar seats in parts of the room that had become customary to them, and to where others of similar disposition clustered. One took wool and needles from her bag and began knitting.

The room had a comfortable, well-used feeling about it. Magazines and newspapers were heaped in small piles on cupboards, along with exercise and text books. A draining board on a sink in the corner was stacked with washed mugs and cups where their owners had rinsed and left them.

The teachers sat in a rough semi-circle around a central wooden table. Jayne Boyle sat to one side, facing them and beside a vacant chair at the centre of the table designated for the Head. There were now around thirty members of staff present, all female, apart from Bryan, with ages ranging from mid twenties to late fifties. Bryan's age group, mid thirties, was predominant and most of the women wore wedding bands. Bryan did not wear a ring. He was joined by Christine. She saw his face, 'What's wrong?'
'HMV! What else – who else! She pisses me off. I mean, *really* pisses me off, big time.'
He explained why. Christine didn't comment. He sensed she agreed with Jayne Boyle on this issue.

The Head came into the staff room. He looked around, nodded briefly at a few teachers, and cleared his throat. The conversation in the quickly room died. Thomas immediately launched into the meeting. After a few routine matters, he raised discipline issues close to him. 'First, mobile phones. It has come to my attention that children are openly flouting our agreed policy.'
Bryan thought of an expression his mother used when confronting him with one of his childish misdeeds: '*a little bird has told me that you…*'
'We need to enforce this. You all know why – or should do by now. The children can abuse these things with bullying

texts and silly pictures. They fiddle around with them in class. And they can be used to parade how well off they are. They can't change the school uniform, so they flaunt these possessions instead.'

Thomas felt himself getting heated, so deliberately stopped, and consulted his notes. If he had his way, he thought, he would hire a steam roller to crush the things to atoms in front of the parents, who had all been assembled to witness the destruction.

'I intend to write – again – to the parents about this. There really is no reason why these things should be brought into school in the first place.'

Bryan thought, '…apart from the bleeding obvious: of parents wanting to be sure that their children are safe.'

'I assume you all agree with this?' the Head concluded, looking carefully at them all.

Jayne looked expectantly toward Bryan. She saw him stir and sit forward in his seat. But he dropped back, his eyes on the carpet, and she knew the moment had passed.

'The other major concern I have is about our recent Diocesan Report. We are deemed 'satisfactory,' which is a polite term for 'unsatisfactory.' He allowed himself a thin smile. There was a polite titter at this cue from the assembled teachers.

Thomas continued, 'The inspection noted that, I quote, "*…the school is committed to providing a strong Catholic*

ethos and sound knowledge of the Catholic faith for all pupils".
'It recognizes,' he continued, 'the leadership changes that have taken place, and notes the work of Jayne, in particular, for her programme monitoring proposals; well done, Jayne.'
Jayne smiled and bowed her head in acknowledgement.
'...It also identifies some interesting attempts at engaging students in class and school assemblies.'

Bryan had been commended by the Inspector for a class assembly involving selected children acting out The Ten Commandments, whilst the rest of the class guessed which one it was. This had been another flash point, as Thomas had discouraged class activities involving role play, in favour of more traditional teacher dominated methods of teaching. Bryan had ignored this, and the Inspectors had spoken at some length to Thomas, extolling the 'effective role play' they had seen in Bryan's class.

'...But the report indicates that teaching is inconsistent across the school, and...'
At that moment a phone trilled, and its owner, red with shame, hurried to the door. 'I'm sorry, my daughter's not well, and my mother is looking after her. This is her now, sorry!'
Thomas ignored her.

'…some older children appear to display a marked lack of interest in the subject. To address this issue, it was suggested that we need to try and involve and engage the parents more in the life of the school so they, hopefully, begin to take more interest in the faith aspect of it. "Building community cohesion" is the term they use; is that a fair summary, Jayne?'

Jayne agreed it was.

'As far as teaching is concerned, Jayne and I will be discussing these issues with Linda, who has agreed to be our R.E. co-ordinator this year, and we will organise a staff training event in due course. Mrs. Dawes, the Inspector, has suggested a teaching approach that looks interesting. However, in the short term, I would be interested in discussing ways we might involve parents more in the school. Any ideas?'

Christine said, 'Parents can be intimidated by school; it's about "well, the kids have got to go, but it's not for the likes of us", that sort of thinking.'

Other teachers nodded their agreement at this.

Christine continued, 'I'd like to propose something the children have been talking about for weeks – ever since they heard that St Winifred's had done it – and that's a Christmas disco for parents, kids, and staff. It could break down the social barriers a bit.'

There was a murmur of assent from most of the teachers.
Christine continued, ‘It’s short notice, but I know someone who could organise this, music, lights; the works. Any volunteers to help me with the food, and decorations to the hall?’
There were some nods from people around her.
Thomas did not warm to the idea, but he judged the mood of the meeting. ‘Thank you, Christine. Would you be willing to take responsibility for this? We would have to agree a budget first, though. I have a Governor’s Meeting this afternoon, so I could raise it then. Can you work out a cost by lunchtime?’
Christine agreed to cost it out. Thomas asked for other ideas to be brought to the next staff meeting and the session was brought to a close.

Chapter Five

Thomas entered the security of his office. He liked the feeling of peace he gained as the door shut behind him. His space. The status of Head-teacher, his. The final decisions - with the Governing Body inevitably endorsing them - his.

The room was square and light, set into the top corner of the building with diagonal views across two playgrounds and the main gate of the school. It was plainly furnished with his desk and executive chair and two hard chairs for visitors. Two filing cabinets and a bookcase, containing education books, were at hand. There was a crucifix above the door and a painting of 'The Last Supper' and some framed professional diplomas on the wall opposite his desk.
He settled to work, and had an hour to prepare for the Governor's meeting and the list of items he wanted them to approve.
**

Mrs. Perry, the School Secretary, brought the tea and biscuits through to a meeting room adjacent to the Head Teacher's office and the Governors settled with their cups and plain digestive biscuits around the table. Thomas, Father Kelly, and Jayne Boyle, were joined by the Chair of Governors, Derek Hartley, a large, florid-faced man, who owned a carpet warehouse in the district, and three others: Harry Bowen, and an Asian man, Ali Desai; and a woman, Margaret Rogers. They were all parents of children at school, and all of a similar middle age and conventional appearance. The school accounts and the Diocesan Report were the main items on the agenda.

Thomas took them through the accounts. It was a constant juggle with income against expenditure for him and the governors, and the Committee were asked to approve a number of expenditure items.

'The staffing bill shows a big increase this year,' commented Derek Hartley.

'Yes, the appointment of learning assistant, Helen Myers, and the yearly salary increase of Bryan Young, because of his Advanced Skills Teacher status, has added a significant amount to our expenditure. We will also need to discuss soon, whether Helen Myers is offered either a second temporary contract, or a permanent contract. But we can defer that to later this term.'

The governors approved spending on repairs to the hall roof and for the purchase of some new computers. They moved on to consider the Diocesan Report. All the governors had been given a copy and Thomas reported on the idea from staff about a disco; Derek Hartley asked for comment.

Ali Desai immediately spoke up, although Thomas had anticipated this in advance in an earlier discussion with Jayne Boyle.

'I am not sure about a disco for encouraging parents to become closer to the school. Can't we do other things – more spiritual? And, as you know, I have raised this issue before about the teaching of other religions in the classroom, and this gives us, the school, a good opportunity to move forward on this. As I have said before, it is good for the children to learn about non-Christian religions too, it will ensure that they…'

Derek Hartley, who had been forewarned by Thomas, moved in quickly. 'Yes, you have raised this before, Ali. Thank you for raising it again. I understand, however, from the Head, that Jayne here will be reviewing the way we teach religious education, and she will report back to us in due course. I'm sure she will take your views into account.' Jayne nodded, 'Of course.'

Father Kelly spoke up. 'On the issue of the disco, I have my reservations too about this, and I will be discussing with the Head other things we can do – a family mass, for example. On your other point, Ali, the children do need to become tolerant of other faiths, of course, but we are a *faith* school – Catholic faith – so this will be, must be, the focus of our spiritual and moral education - as Islam would be in a

Muslim school. Most parents with children here want their children to become good Catholics.'
Harry Bowen nodded in agreement. 'Yes, that's why my children are here.'
'Yes, yes, of course, and I am happy with the school generally, and my daughter can learn about Islam from me and my wife, this is true, but in good Muslim schools the children are taught about other faiths. This is a good opportunity for the school…a good chance for the children to learn respect for other beliefs…I would really like to see other faith representatives coming into the school – I know an Imam that would be happy to come here and…
Derek Hartley took a grip. 'Yes, thank you, Ali! As I say, I'm sure Jayne will be looking at all these issues in her review. Were there any other comments about this report? I notice that some of the staff received particular praise for their work.'
Margaret Rogers plucked up courage to speak. 'I read that Mr. Young was praised.' She had a daughter in Bryan's class and had heard about the Ten Commandments role play.
Thomas said, 'I was pleased that our colleagues were praised by the Inspectors. Mrs. Kingston received some very positive comments and recognition for her work with the younger children; as did Mrs.Clough. And of course, Jayne here was commended for her leadership.'

Jayne smiled at him and acknowledged the encouraging nods from the Governors.
'Your leadership, too,' said Derek.
'Thank you, Derek,' said Thomas.
**

Bryan saw Latesha's mother waiting for her at the gate.
'What's she done now?' Latesha's mother, Grace, was a large, harassed looking woman in her forties.
Bryan explained about the incident in the classroom. 'I don't want to go to the Head with this. Is everything OK with her at home?'
'No, not really. She's been a little cow lately. I told you before, about when she was at the other school: the name calling, because her real dad is Black – that's why we transferred her here. It was alright at first, but she's been pushing her sister around at home lately. It's like she's had a taste of bullying - on the receiving end - so she's getting in first now; she likes the taste of it herself.'
'Anything triggered it off?' Bryan asked.
Grace hesitated. 'She's been unsettled with…with Tom moving in, and that. But that's the only thing I can think of. He don't stand no nonsense from her, and tells her off. But she don't like it when he does. I can understand it, I wouldn't have done at her age either, but that's the price you got to pay. He's got a good job.'

Chapter Six

Bryan rode home on his bicycle. He lived a couple of miles from the school in a terraced house, close to one of the stations that connected the district to central London. He had been born in the area and his parents had lived there all their lives. He had been at the house since his appointment at Holy Apostles, nearly three years ago. At the same time, he had been joined by his girl-friend, Jennifer, now his partner, and in the last eighteen months by Adam, their son.

He had left secondary school at sixteen with not much to show for his indifferent time there, apart from a strong flair for English, and had drifted from job to job, until he had decided to go back to college as a mature student. As a part of his course he had done some work experience in a primary school helping the kids to read, and realized he liked it and had a gift for teaching. The kids liked his easy, jokey style, and he found he was tuned into their daft ways and sympathetic to their natural tendencies to say 'no' to anyone who told them they should say 'yes.'

He had studied for an education degree, with a specialism in teaching English in primary schools and been a teacher now for ten years; The Holy Apostles was his second appointment. He was drawn to the school because it was in 'special measures' at the time, and for the chance to help pull it around. As a child he had gone to St. Winifred's, the other Catholic primary school in the district, but he knew The Holy Apostles and how it had sunk; he had heard the kids had been out of control, until the Head decided enough was enough and retired back to his native Devon.

It was Bryan's first Catholic school appointment, as the previous one had not been affiliated to any particular church. Bryan had been baptized a Catholic but had gradually drifted away from attending church, although he still retained a belief of sorts in…something…God? He had been quizzed at the selection interview by the governors at The Holy Apostles about his beliefs, and had remembered enough from his own education to say the right things about religion. They had asked him too about his marital status; he was in his thirties, and he could read the doubt in their eyes about him – a single man; in a primary school? But he assured them that he was in a 'steady relationship – with a woman – and 'was discussing marriage' with her - a lie, but he wanted the job. He explained that his current single status was because of his early unsettled career, and carefully refrained from expressing his non-commitment, in common with many of his former college friends, to the conventions of marriage.

He had met Jennifer at college. She was studying graphic design, and they had gone around together. He was drawn to the mixture of creativity and order in her personality. She was imaginative and inventive, but in a controlled and organised way that complemented an undisciplined seam in his nature. He liked her trim figure, her style of dress, and the way her elfin-style fair hair contrasted with his own black unruly mop. She had a mocking way about her that punctured his ego whenever it swelled; but he did not resent this - on the contrary he admired her honesty, and knew he needed someone to do this to and for him. When they graduated, they went their separate ways for a while: Jennifer into a studio in London as an illustrator; he into his first school appointment.

But they kept in touch. They both made good progress in their careers and spent more and more time together in their respective rented flats.

When Bryan was appointed at The Holy Apostles, on a higher salary, they decided to buy a house together. It was a solid, comfortable property, and together they had decorated it in styles that drew on each other's personalities and tastes. The furniture and carpeting was Jennifer's choice: fashionable; soft, autumnal colours; good quality. Bryan had filled the walls with colour: posters, paintings found at car

boot sales, and copies of framed prints that Jennifer had produced for her clients.
Their independent lives had worked well together; each revolving in its own sphere during the working day, to merge with pleasure for a few hours each evening and on their free days.

Their child had not been planned, but his arrival in its embryonic form, at least, had at first unnerved, then pleased them. Eighteen months on, Adam, the toddler, still touched the core of their being, but his life had changed theirs in a way that caused them to stamp down feelings of resentment that lurked in the shadows.
They were unmarried partners; nothing extraordinary in this, and the norm in their peer group. But at another emotional level they were both still single - and both still with a lingering sense of independence. But at an even deeper level, moral echoes from their childhood – both children of parents strictly conformist in their own ways – still reverberated. Jennifer's parents - both still alive - were quietly unhappy in their unspoken disappointment at her unmarried status. They did not come much to the house; she went to theirs. They loved their grandchild, but worried for his future, and for Jennifer. They felt her arrangement with Bryan was fragile; there was, they felt, something intangible about him, but they kept their own counsel on this.

Bryan's own parents would have called his situation "living in sin". He was not sure that he would have had the courage to enter into this arrangement when they had been alive; he could not have easily faced and presented them, his mother in particular, with what they would have regarded as a bastard grandchild. Now they were dead, a part of him enjoyed feeling unconventional and kicking against the faith of his baptism. But a nagging voice reminded him of his Catholicism and the strictures of the Church on morality and the importance of marriage. For this reason, he kept his life outside school closed to most of his colleagues. Only Christine at the school knew of his situation, and she kept a discreet silence. But others had suspicions. Once, out shopping, with Adam in a buggy, they had met another teacher from school. Bryan did not say 'this is my wife'; he just said, 'this is Jennifer and Adam,' and had left the teacher to draw her own conclusions about the nature of the relationship. This she did, and soon the information was passed around the staff room, a mental note of the situation quietly taken by Jayne Boyle.

He opened the street door. Adam came stumbling toward him. He scooped the child up, and greeted Jennifer, 'How's it been?'

She was tired. She was also unkempt: there were stains on her skirt and her hair needed cutting. Since having Adam, she worked at home with projects sent to her from the studio. But she missed the regular social contact with her colleagues and the opportunity this gave to dress and groom for the occasion.

'Not too bad, although I'm feeling it now. I managed to get an hours work done when he was asleep this morning, and a bit more this afternoon, but some idiot selling something rang the bell and woke him up, so I had to break off. He's been all over the place and wanting attention. He can't concentrate on anything for more than two minutes, so I can't draw for long. He's either wanting me to play with him, or wandering off somewhere. It was too wet to go far today.'

Bryan was tired too, and felt his irritation rising. He wanted to ignore the sounds of complaints; wanted to hear other things, but realized this was his life now. The prospect of having a golden child, when you were childless, was different from the noisy, shitting, intrusive reality when it actually arrived. Neither had really anticipated the physical toll of looking after a small child who could now move around, throw things as it went, pick up bleach bottles, and stick its fingers into contraptions that snapped back at them. Others said, 'they'll soon grow up'. But they missed the bit out: about how it happens one grinding day at a time.

Jennifer was working on some book illustrations and the deadline was fast approaching. 'I'll have to put in an extra hour or two tonight.'

They had got into a routine of having tea together, and then Bryan would look after Adam, play with him for a while, and then put him to bed. Jennifer would work on her illustrations and join him later in the evening for an hour to unwind before bed. Adam was waking regularly in the night, and by taking turns at going to him, it shared the burden, but at the cost of sleep for both of them.

Over tea, with the child playing nearby, Bryan talked about his day. He told her of the incident in the classroom with Thomas. 'I don't know why he is such a prick,' he said. Jennifer had recovered her equilibrium. 'Two cocks in the hen-house,' she commented, 'maybe that's his problem – and yours? You told me he is a good teacher, in his own way, maybe you want to be the top cock?'
He thought about this; but it wasn't about him wanting to be Head. He wasn't bothered about management. He would be hopeless at it, and he was on a decent salary now anyway. It was Thomas, the man.

Bryan recognized that Thomas had pulled the school out of the pit it had fallen into. The school was now a popular one with local parents, although before Thomas had been appointed it had been in serious trouble with the government inspection team, who had put it into what was known as 'special measures,' due to the previous head teacher who had let discipline slide. Thomas had pulled it round, and the inspectors had recently judged it 'good,' He had done it by recognizing the skills of individual teachers and making them specialists in the subjects they liked and taught best. They all managed their own classes, but would also share their skills and ensure that the work set across the school matched the abilities of the children. This gave them all extra responsibilities, but it was better and more effective than expecting teachers to be good at teaching everything. Thomas had also organized the House system, and homework had been reintroduced. The wearing of school uniform was strictly enforced, temporary tattoos and jewellery banned, and the non-attendance of children strictly followed-up by the school or by the education welfare service. Thomas had introduced voluntary additional reading schemes and had encouraged volunteers from the community into the school to listen to the children read.

All good - but he didn't like the man. Thomas discouraged teaching ideas that gave children too much opportunity, for, as he put it, 'free expression.' He preferred that they learn the basics of reading, writing and numbers under the firm direction of a teacher, who set the agenda and was clear about what the children should learn, and how it could be measured. He expected his teachers to fall in line with him on this, but Bryan resisted; he argued that the children needed more, not fewer, opportunities to learn in a free-ranging way, such as with drama, debate and role play. This had led them into increasingly acrimonious discussions, both in and outside of staff meetings. The situation had grown worse since the incident with the book.

Bryan, in his role as literacy coordinator for the school, had been given the task of liaison with teachers and selecting books for the different levels of ability in the school. For the older children, one of the books he had recommended was '*How we are born*', about conception and birth. This one had colour illustrations of a naked couple: woman complete with breasts and pubic hair, and a man with dangling cock, standing with their arms around each other. In a boxed section later the book had explained, but not illustrated, how the man's penis became 'hard,' which showed he 'was excited to be with the woman,' and how this led to the man being able to 'enter his penis into the womb of the woman.'

This had led to Thomas confronting Bryan and the first of a number of conversations, similar to the one he'd had today, about 'loss of innocence' of the children, and confronting them 'too soon' with the realities of life. Bryan had defended the book; it had been used successfully in other schools as part of personal and development studies, and it gave children, he argued, honest detail in a clear and non-prurient way on a topic they half-knew about anyway. But Father Kelly had objected to the fact that the couple depicted in the book were 'in a loving relationship,' but with no mention of marriage. Thomas had taken the matter to a staff meeting, and although a number sided with him, including Jayne Boyle, who felt this type of information should be coming from parents, the majority supported Bryan's position. The book was bought, but the chilled relationship between the two men worsened.

'He's got a poker up his arse,' said Bryan. 'He can control a class all right, and he knows his subject, but he's an Android. I wouldn't be surprised if he was dropped off by Martians on Rainham Marshes to infiltrate us! The kids are wary of him!'

'Not like you then, 'Mr. Popular,' 'Mr. King-Cool'!' Jennifer was aware of some heat, as well as light, in her feelings behind her comments. 'If you are head-honcho, maybe you need to set the agenda and stick to it.'

'No, he's definitely programmed to spout the New Testament when confronted with earthly wickedness.'

Maybe that's it, thought Bryan, why Thomas irritated him so much. The Head reminded him of those earnest types who travelled in pairs, banging on your door when you were watching a decent television programme, to tell you that they had 'good news' for you. He usually said he was a Quaker to get rid of them. Telling them you were a Catholic didn't do the trick these days, as they usually launched into solemn-faced rants about the Pope, paedophile priests, and child abuse scandals.

'It's more than that. I think you are still bothered about who you are, and your working-class origins. You're just not comfortable with those in authority!'

Bryan recognized the truth in this. Thomas had the accent and superior bearing of the middle class teachers he remembered from his own school days. He felt that these teachers may have wanted, and spouted, social equality whilst at university, but when faced with the working classes en-masse behaving badly and giving the finger to education, they gradually lost their social optimism, barely concealed their sneers, and accentuated their diction to lay down their middle-class rules to the proles .

Jennifer's remarks about a man in the hen-house struck him, too. He was quite comfortable working with women, and he liked the kids. He got on with their mothers, but found it harder to relate to their fathers. In the district, men, if they worked, were either in manual jobs or in places where there was a mix of men and women. Bryan felt that the fathers weren't sure what to make of a man who worked with children as a full-time career. When he met fathers at parent's evenings he found himself emphasising and deepening his local accent and working-class mannerisms to show he was one of them.

After tea, Jennifer retreated to her study to carry on with her work and Bryan turned his attention to his son.

**

Tracy Banks watched her mum get ready. Della Banks pursed her lips at the mirror as she applied her lipstick.

'Where you going?' asked Tracy.

'Out. I've asked Carol to come over and sit. But I want you in bed by ten.' Della plumped up her hair and adjusted the drop of her skirt to show off her knees.

'Who you going with?'

'Tony, if you must know.'

Tracy frowned, 'is he staying over again?'

'I don't know. And it's none of your business anyway!'

'I don't know what you see in him. He's fat.'

Della flared. 'Do you want a slap? You're asking for one, I'll tell you that!'

'Why don't you go out with someone decent? I know someone - and he ain't married', said Tracy.

‘Look you, I won’t tell you again, this ain’t your concern. You’ve got too much to say for yourself my lady! Now listen, I don’t want you watching telly all night. You got homework? And your tea just needs to go into the microwave for five minutes. Shelley’s had hers. Who do you know anyway?’

‘It’s Mr. Young, at school. He’s nice. There’s a picture of him in that school report.’

Della regarded herself again in the mirror. She remembered the picture. ‘Is he the one with the floppy black hair? I suppose it must be; he’s the only bloke there, apart from the head man.’

‘Yeah. Tanya’s mum said she fancies him.’

‘What’s an unmarried teacher his age doing teaching kids your age? He’s probably a poofter.’

‘No he ain’t! Tanya said she saw him with a woman once in the Mall, but he don’t wear a ring or anything, and he don’t say anything about a wife. We keep asking him, but he won’t say anything about it.’

‘Who’s that?’ asked Shelley, Tracy’s older sister, who came into the room eating a lump of bread.

‘Mind your own business!' said Tracy.

‘Who’s she on about, mum?’

‘Some teacher at school. Mr. Young, or ‘Yum-Yum,’ by the sound of it.’

They all laughed. 'Mr. Yum-Yum. I'll have to call him that,' said Tracy.
'Yeah, he's alright. We had him for English last year before I left. He's better than that stuck-up Woody-Woodpecker' said Shelley, 'You can have a laugh with him.'
'You can meet him, mum, at the disco,' said Tracy.
'What disco? This is the first I've heard about it.'
'The school is having a disco for everyone, teachers an' all.'
'What the bleeding hell for?'
'I dunno, but you'll have to come, mum, all the other girls' mums are going. You will, won't you?'
'We'll see. Right! Don't forget, I want you in bed when I get back.'

Chapter Seven

Jayne Boyle opened the door of her mother's house. All the lights were, as usual blazing, but it was as cold as a morgue. It was a rented house, and the council had installed central heating a year or so earlier, but her mother, Alice, kept the thermostat low, relying instead on her wool cardigans and single gas fire in the main room for heating. Alice had grown up at a time when coal fires were the norm and had got used to low temperatures. But to Jayne - who had moved into her own home after graduating - her mother's house felt arctic. If she attempted to raise the temperature, her mother would fan herself with a newspaper and lower the thermostat on her next lavatory trip.

Bracing herself mentally, Jayne went into the front room where her mother sat. 'I'm back,' she said, 'had a good day?'

'These glasses aren't right,' said her mother.

Jayne's spirits plummeted, 'What's wrong with them?'

'I can't read properly. The words all blur. And they've been stinking the house up again with their cooking.'

'They' were the young Asian couple who had moved in next door, and immediately upset Alice by building a summer house in their garden. The house had originally been owned by the council, but had been bought by the then tenants, to be sold on a few years later. This had been the norm in the road where Alice lived, until she was one of just a handful of council tenants remaining.

'Noise and dirt everywhere! The builders don't speak English - or pretend not to. I went out to them today. They keep dropping dirt over the fence. They just stood there looking at me as if I was doolally: "no speak, no speak". They'll all be illegal immigrants, doing it on the cheap. I'm sick of it. I've a good mind to report them. They won't have planning permission.'

Jayne tried to change the topic of conversation before Alice used more racist language, which would invariably lead them into an argument.

'Maybe you need to get used to them a bit more. You've only just got them. They said it takes time for your eyes to adjust.'

'No! I'm taking them back. I've paid a fortune for these frames. I knew that girl wasn't interested.'

Jayne felt a familiar oppressive weight. It meant she would have to organise a trip to take her mother back to the opticians. Her mother was confined in the house all day with nothing to do but get herself into turmoil over the multitude of things that vexed her. Alice read, and did crosswords, and liked to hobble on her frame around her small garden that Jayne now tended for her. But in the winter she could not move beyond her rooms, and so got irritated with everything, including herself. The day was punctuated by a pill-taking routine to alleviate all her ailments, notably painful arthritis in hips and knees, a heart condition, and depression - although she had convinced herself that the latter were to help her sleep.

Since her husband, Tom, had died, Alice had become increasingly frail and vulnerable. Jayne had taken the decision a year or so ago to rent out her own flat and to care for Alice in the family home, rather than seek a council-run care institution, which would have seen the swift end of her mother. But the decision was taking its toll; by degrees, she was losing control of her life outside of school. A visit to the opticians on Saturday would deprive Jayne of a weekend chance to escape and walk alone by the river for a few hours.

Sundays saw a break to Alice's routine when Jayne took her mother to Mass, where her mother metamorphosed in the company of slightly younger parishioners - who treated her like their favourite aunt. Jayne, the dutiful, but unmarried only child, would be greeted with a few thin smiles, whilst her mother would sit in her usual place and greet benignly those who came to pay respectful homage to her.
'Alice, how are you dear?' one would say, kissing Alice warmly on both cheeks and holding her hands.
'Mustn't grumble; all's well. How are you, dear?' Alice would give the appearance of listening, tilting and nodding

her head benevolently to the forthcoming tale of woe, although she missed most of it because of her deafness, 'I'll pray for you, dear. God's good,' she would say.

'I'll get our tea ready,' said Jayne.
'Don't give me any of that Jewish stuff again.'
'It's not Jewish. It's called Kohl Rabi, it's like turnip.'
'I don't know why you bought it.'
'I wanted to try it for a change.'
'Well, I didn't like it!'
During tea, Jayne tried to get her mother back to better humour.
'Any cards today?'
Alice brightened. 'Eight! I've got nearly fifty now. There's one from across the road. I'll get you to take one over later for me.'
Alice's Christmas cards were spread across the mantelpiece and sideboard. 'I wrote a few more today. I'll get you to post them when you go over. You got one. It's from abroad.'
After tea, Jayne looked at her card. It was from a pen friend and she placed it alongside the other six in her allocated corner of the room. She retreated to her room to mark the children's work, read her *Catholic Herald*, and be on her own.
**

Thomas and his wife, Isabel, sat down to their meal. He had opened a bottle of Chardonnay. 'How was your day?' Isabel enquired. She had been a teacher too, and had reached a deputy headship post before taking early retirement, although she still did some teaching supply work. He summarised his day, but lingered over his encounter with Bryan.

'I know he has ability. But there's an attitude about him - something sneering that I can't abide. He encourages the children in their disrespect… well, not exactly encourages it, but it's more that he doesn't discourage it. It's hard to explain'

He thought hard to find the correct words, '…he encourages liberties that can undermine discipline.'

'I'm not sure I follow. How does he do that?'

'It's about…about allowing himself to be too easy going with the children. He is too…too familiar with them.'

'How do you mean 'familiar'? Do you mean in a sinister way?'

'No, no, no, nothing like that. But effective teaching to me is about keeping your distance with children. A teacher should be someone the children can go to, of course, but not like some jokey uncle, who wants to be your best friend. There needs to be some…*balance*…some *distance*, call it respect, otherwise they… or some, at least, will take advantage, especially at this school.'

'Does he have problems keeping control in the class?'
'No, he doesn't have discipline problems,' he said grudgingly.
'The children like him?'
'Yes, but as I say, too much, I think.'

Thomas remembered his time at teacher training college. There was a male teacher there, just like Bryan Young, always spouting ideas about giving children 'space and freedom to learn.' The college tutors all liked him, and they all went to the pub together, familiar and easy in each other's company, swopping anecdotes.
But he had overheard two of the same tutors talking about him: 'Wood by name - and by nature' said one, and the other laughed in agreement.
So be it. The comments had determined him to throw himself into his work, to advance in his career on his knowledge, ability, and determination. If people did not like him, he would ensure they would respect him.
He had climbed slowly through the ranks of the profession, taking on the extra responsibilities, going to conferences, putting the hours in, doing things right, properly. No gimmicks in the classroom, no razzmatazz; instead, steady effort. 'Reading, not role play' was his motto for what constituted effective learning and teaching. He regarded himself as a 'safe pair of hands' - and a good Catholic -

which, he heard later, had swung things his way at the Selection Board for his first headship at The Holy Apostles. Being male in a primary school was also a help, as it set him apart from the other candidates; a fact he had emphasised at his interview: 'Male role model…married, two children doing well in their careers…shows the boys what can be achieved. Even in a Catholic school, some of these children, sadly, don't have a father figure around…'

'Do the children like you?' one of the interviewers had asked.

He had felt the flutter of hesitation. 'I have always tried to earn respect as a good teacher. Good results for the children mean, in the long term, good career prospects for them. That's more important than liking. Their parents know this.'

Did they like him? Some did, he felt sure of that, particularly the brighter ones who were keen to learn, and whom he nurtured, although most were quiet, or hesitant, in his presence. But he put the measure of his success in their advancement: at their progress in reading and using numbers, showing respect to others, and learning how to compromise. His school performance results spoke for themselves now: from below to now around the national average in Maths and English, and rising. To keep a school in this position meant all its teachers in it working as a team – without challenge to the team leader.

Chapter Eight

December: The Feast of Blessed Thomas Somers

The hall had been decorated with streamers and multi-coloured balloons; a 'Cool-Cats Christmas Disco' banner, complete with dancing cats drawn by Christine and her class, fluttered above the stage. The hall chairs and lunch tables had been folded and pushed to the edges of the hall, and just inside the hall door was a trestle table covered with plates of buffet food and plastic bottles of water. Christine and a small group of mothers had worked all afternoon preparing the food, and the children starting to arrive flocked around it. 'Not yet! Look, but don't touch. Food is for later,' said Christine.

It was warm in the hall, and on the stage a middle-aged man, the DJ, was adjusting the volume on his speaker system. He bobbed his shoulders to the music as he worked, and a bald patch, red with a fresh scab and glistening with sweat, shone through his flowing locks. A familiar disco tune began to increase the palpable tempo in the room, and some of the children, jumping up and down with excitement, began to look for partners. Small circles of girls were bobbing and weaving around each other, whilst boys formed noisy groups on the edge of the floor, pushing each other towards the girls. The disc-jockey set strobe lighting beams around the room in time to the music, increasing the excitement; Christine dimmed the main lights.

The half-light emphasised the exotic appearance of the children. The younger girls were in their party dresses, but the older ones, of nine and ten, were transformed into pre-women in imitation of their current television idols. Hair was pinned-up and decorated with gold and silver clips; eyes were dark with mascara, cheeks rouged, lips painted. All were wearing their most expensive clothes, many newly bought for the occasion: some with mini-skirts and sparkling tops, others with tight, slinky trousers and half jumpers that showed their bare midriffs; one girl had a pierced belly-button and wore a gold ring through it.

They were conscious of each other, and showed off their bracelets, hair decorations and necklaces. The prohibition on temporary tattoos had been lifted for the evening – much against Thomas's instincts - and some girls made a point of displaying these now on their calves or shoulders – flowers, snakes, Ying and Yang symbols.

The boys were self-consciously dressed in jeans, sweat-shirts, or denim tops, many with hair standing in spiky peaks, stiff with hair gel. Some wore chunky gold or silver chains around their chests or necks, and their eyes swept the floor to inspect and compare footwear. One nine year old boy sported a pair of reflective lens sunglasses and adopted an insouciant air, hands in pockets, as he indifferently watched the girls dance. Another wore all black: black jacket, shirt, trousers, shoes with spats, and a black trilby hat, cut low over his eyes.

A favourite disco tune brought a group of girls together in a line as they danced in formation to the insistent beat, their arms swaying above their heads as they moved together, three steps forward, one back, two sideways, clap. Gradually, the boys filtered onto the floor to dance, together at first, on the fringes of the girls, until slowly boys and girls merged, mostly dancing in small groups of two and three. The more conspicuously dressed gravitated centrally to each other, and to the middle of the floor, so that their gold and silver decorations flashed and glinted in the strobe lighting, whilst the children in plainer garb were edged to the sides of the hall.

The parents and teachers had also arrived and stood in small groups. The mothers outnumbered fathers by around three to one, and everyone had made an effort to look smart, some of the mothers mirroring the glamorous outfits of their daughters.

Jayne Boyle arrived and immediately felt self-conscious in her print dress. There was no obvious person she could go to easily for company, so she went to the food table and started to rearrange the plates into more formal patterns, pies with pies, cakes with cakes, pizzas into circles. She felt sneering eyes on her and with relief saw that the Head and Father Kelly had arrived. She went across and greeted them both.

'How is it going, Jayne?'

'As you see.'

All three looked on in silence. Father Kelly said, 'It's too late to start with a prayer, I suppose?'

'Yes,' said Thomas, 'Far too late.'

Tracy arrived with Della and raced off to join a group of girls from her class in the centre of the hall. She was wearing an expensive dress in vivid red, its flared bottom swinging above her thin knees. The skirt, festooned with glass beading, sparkled in the light, and a long, black necklace swung on her neck. Her hair was pinned up, with a decorated pigtail falling down from the crown. Her cheeks were rouged, and she had painted her stubby, bitten nails to match the colour of her dress. She bounced around the others in the centre of the hall.

Della was wearing a black Jersey and lace shift dress that emphasized her figure. She recognized Cheryl, Tanya's mum, and went across to join her, noting with quiet satisfaction Cheryl's swelling hips and backside, straining for release from the under-sized and cheap dress she wore. 'Hello Cheryl. Nice dress!' Cheryl detected the note of derision in Della's voice, but ignored it. 'You too, Della. You alright?' she replied, coolly.

Mothers began to join their children in the dancing, and gradually teachers were drawn into the middle. Helen, the teaching assistant, wore a tight black dress, cut low at the front. Charlie and his mates gathered round her.
'Cor! You look alright, Miss. Where's your boyfriend?'
'I thought you were my boyfriend, Charlie!'
'I wouldn't mind. Come on, Miss, have a dance.'
Helen began to dance in time to the music and Charlie and the other boys circled around her. She lined them up after a while and they began to copy her easy forward, back and turn movements. Most were self-conscious and moved robotically, but Charlie tuned into the music and relaxed.
'You're a good dancer, Charlie; good dancers always get the girls!' Helen said. He blushed with pleasure.

Della and Tracy, and a group of other mothers and daughters, swayed and bobbed together in a group.

Tracy noticed Bryan come into the hall. 'Mum! There's that Mr. Young I told you about.'
Della looked across at him. 'I've seen worse. Not bad - for a teacher.'
Bryan was wearing his black leather jacket, hipster jeans, and tee-shirt. He made a stark contrast with Thomas, standing nearby, wearing grey flannel trousers, white shirt and tie, and a blue M&S pullover.
Cheryl said, 'I wouldn't mind a bit of tuition from him.'
Della laughed. 'Yeah, that's our Mr. Yum-Yum. Well, I wouldn't say no either. I could probably give him some in return!'

Christine joined Bryan. 'How's it going?' he asked.
'It's good. The kids are really enjoying it; the parents too, by the look of it.'
He looked across at the trio by the door. 'Do you think we can persuade Jayne and Thomas to lead a conga around the room?'
Christine laughed, 'Or Father Kelly to do a limbo, with the other two holding the pole?'
They looked at the dancers, and enjoyed what they saw.
'Are you having a dance, or what?' Christine asked Bryan.
'I'll settle for the 'what.' I'm starving. I haven't had any tea.'

Christine had a word with the disc-jockey and he brought the music to a halt. She raised the lights and shouted, 'Come and have some refreshments.'

Father Kelly made a step forward with the intention of saying Grace, but the children surged past him, their parents close behind, and surrounded the table in a noisy, jostling crowd. Food was scooped up and both children and parents retreated to chairs at the side of the hall.

Bryan got a plate and began to pile it with food. He found himself looking at Della, who was standing next to him with an empty plate.

'Handsome,' she said to him.

'O, thank you very much.'

'Not you! The pizza,' she said, 'Hand some over.'

'I see. The pizza's got more appeal. Charming!'

'Yeah, it'll do for the main course. We'll have to see what's on offer for afters.'

He looked appraisingly at her. Della was eyeing him coolly, a half-smile on her face.

'I don't think we've met before.'

'I'm Tracy's mum. She's in your class this year. I haven't met you before. I couldn't get to the last Parent's Evening. You know our Shelley, too. She was in Mrs. Healey's class before she went onto the Sacred Heart. You'd only just started teaching here then.'

Bryan felt a mild sense of disappointment. Tracy had become a nuisance this year by demanding attention, and he sensed that most other children found her too pushy and noisy, even for this school.

'How's she doing?'

'OK. Yeah. Lively. She keeps me on my toes.'

'Is that teacher-speak, for "she's a pain in the backside"?'

'No, she's alright really, although she's bringing her phone into school lately. I see she's got it with her tonight, too. The Head's not happy about phones in school.'

'No! Go on!' Della said, 'Well! There's a thing; Mr. Wood not happy!'

Bryan grinned. 'It's Bryan, by the way.'

'Della.'

They stood in comfortable silence until they were joined in a whirling rush by Tracy and two other girls.

'Hello Sir. Don't my mum look sexy and cool?'

Bryan was caught unawares. 'Yes, she does. So do you, Tracy. What a cool dress.'

Tracy bounced around in joy and the music began again.

'Come on Mum, come on Sir, let's all dance!'

Della looked at him and raised an eyebrow. Bryan felt himself stir with more than just friendly interest in a pupil and her parent. His sex life with Jennifer had shrunk over the last six months, both sucked slowly dry by Adam and his night-time wailing.

They all moved into the centre and began to move in time to the music. The flashing silver light rippled down Della, throwing swift and fleeting shadows across her face and intensifying the jet of her hair. Her body flowed, loose and easy, to the music, her eyes fixed on him.
He had an easy grace when dancing, the light reflecting on the leather of his coat, and they began to consciously match and mirror each other in the gradual abandon of their movements. The tempo of the music increased; she felt her herself consciously slipping free from the tensions of the day. A gossamer of sweat frosted the top of her lip as she moved, her body, curving and shaping into the music.
Her hair fell around her face, whipped across it, then back, the dark of her eyes momentarily lightened by the darting lights. Bryan too, felt himself loosening, unravelling; a damp patch of perspiration darkened his tee-shirt and spread slowly down to his navel.

'What's Bryan's situation, Jayne? Is he married?
Jayne Boyle turned to the Head. 'Well, he doesn't talk about it. But I heard he was seen in town with a woman who was pushing a child in a buggy. But I don't know who she was.

I think she probably was 'a partner' ' - she emphasized the word - 'at least, that was the impression of Marjorie who bumped into them. He's on his own tonight, so I don't really know.'
'He seems very familiar with Tracy's mother, and the child seems quite besotted with him.'

Tracy and two of her friends had fallen in line with Bryan and Della, mimicking each other's movements: hands on hips, one leg forward, sway, sway, sway, jump, turn to the side, clap. Tracy shrieked with laughter at each jump, her eyes fixed on Bryan.

Jayne said, 'Yes, besotted. You may be right about that.' She told the Head about the children's 'love' and 'hate' writing, and what Tracy had written. Thomas looked carefully at her, nodding his interest.
'You can open a Pandora's Box, if you're not careful,' Thomas said.
'Yes, that's what I said to him, too.'
They looked at each other and smiled.

Bryan stood outside the school hall with Della and Tracy. The disco was over, the lights back on. Thomas had thanked the parents for attending and hoped he would see more of them at Parent's Evenings. Christine, Jayne and a few other teachers started to collect the remnants of the food and stack the plates. Jim, the school caretaker, moved in with his broom. Children, parents and teachers now streamed out in friendly groups into the night, the children still excited, and some still dancing together. Father Kelly stood at the door nodding to everyone, hoping he would see them at Mass on Sunday.

Della and Bryan stood looking at each other. 'Well, that was nice,' said Della. 'You're not a bad dancer – for a teacher!'
'I wasn't born a teacher. I used to cut it at Kingsley Hall on a Saturday night before I went to college.'
'Did you, my, my! It's all coming out now. Kingsley Hall…what next! '
They both laughed. Kingsley Hall was regarded as a sad Saturday night venue that you only went to in desperation, when nothing else was happening. He looked at Della and felt a lingering ripple of interest as she wrapped her fur-lined coat around her body. She saw him looking, and shook her hair loose of the collar; it flicked and bobbed in the breeze. She met his gaze and held it.
Tracy ran up and grabbed his arm; she swung around on it. 'Sir, Sir, let me take a photo! She produced her phone camera. 'Let me take one of you both.'

Bryan felt a vague sense of doubt, but Della merely shrugged, 'She's mad about the camera; takes pictures of everybody.'
They stood side by side. 'Put your arms round each other,' commanded Tracy.
Bryan laughed and shook his head. 'What would Mr. Wood say, Tracy!'
Della laughed too, and half turned to look at him. She thought, 'I could do with your arms around me', as she saw him close up, dishevelled, and with sweat still translucent on his face. He looked at her, and had the same thought. The flash from Tracy's camera lit up their faces.
**

He still had the image of Della in his mind as he as he opened the door. The acid tang of warm piss and vomit hit him immediately. Jennifer appeared cradling a grizzling Adam.
'He won't go off!' she said, her voice at a high pitch, close to tears. 'He's been throwing up for the last hour. I didn't know if I should call the doctor. I couldn't do any work; I'm miles behind, and I'm running a cold, I can feel it coming on.'
Adam had vomited on her jumper.

Bryan immediately felt guilty at leaving her to go to the disco, and for the prick of lust for another woman; the image of Della still fresh in his mind.
'I'll take him'. He took Adam, who howled louder and reached out for his mother. She sank down into a chair, her nose dripping, 'Had a good time?' she said. Her tone put him on the defensive.
'You know I had to go. I didn't have much choice,' he said, his temper rising. The toddler continued his howling, the noise drilling into his head, stirring his anger. He felt like shaking them both.
She put her head into her hands and the sobs came, racking her body in spasms, increasing his guilt, and his temper.
She poured out her frustration of being stuck in the house, of doing all the work. He didn't help her. He didn't do the jobs she had asked him a dozen times to do, like mend the drip on the bathroom tap. They didn't go anywhere…not interested in her anymore…just talked about his work.
He gritted his teeth and prowled back and forth with the child, whose howls continued unabated.

Bryan lay awake in bed. Jennifer lay away from him, edged close to her side of the bed. The tension hung in the room, its silent presence denying them both sleep, whilst the clock marked its slow, indifferent passage through the night. He knew he should put his arm across her shoulders and say soft words. But he didn't, he couldn't. The image of Della: glamorous, raven haired, smiling Della, played with him, and followed him down into a half sleep, until he woke abruptly feeling a damp warmth spreading across his pyjama bottoms.

Chapter Nine

December: The Feast of St. Lucy

Bryan locked his cycle and noticed with amusement that the older children were still in a disco mood. They were showing off their group dance steps, the girls 'la-la-lahing' the words of a popular song. Tracy spotted him, 'Come and join in, Sir.'

'No, no, I've got to get ready for first class.'

'O come on, Sir,' the children cried, 'you're a good dancer!' Tracy and another girl grabbed his hands and pulled him into their group.

'Come on, Sir. Show us what you can do. Father Kelly said he'd have a turn with us!' said one boy, to the laughter of the other children.

The boy, encouraged, said, 'Can you imagine him! His great fat belly shaking about, blob, blob!' He grabbed hold of his stomach and pretended to shake it up and down.

The children rocked with laughter. Bryan suppressed his grin and pretended not to notice, as the boy stomped around like Falstaff.

More girls came running up. A line of six girls now showed off their line dancing steps, the others clapping and humming the tune. Bryan wanted to join in and show them his dancing prowess. He tagged on to the end of the line,

easily copying the movements of the others. They encouraged him: 'ain't he good.'
And he felt good, easy, relaxed with the kids; they were doing what kids always did, harmless stuff; a bit of anarchy, disorder was OK. There was time enough to be constrained by life when you had to get a job, but try telling that to the Head and to HMV. And he was glad to be free of the house, with its post-row silence still leaden.
He exaggerated his movements, showing off, taking the lead away from the girls. The other dancers fell in with the new steps he was using. Tracy had slipped away from the group and was filming the scene on her camera phone.
**

It was the reading hour. The children could pick any book and sit and read it, whilst Bryan slowly went around the room listening to them. He always started by encouraging them to read on their own, then about half way through the class he would allow them to read to each other in small groups if they wished, and most did.
He believed this encouraged the abilities of both the stronger and weaker children, although he needed to keep a tight grip on the class to keep them focused. The boys, predictably, had picked books about bloody or fast-moving things, and some were already pointing out the more colourful plates to the others on their tables.

‘It took three chops to cut off her head,’ said Charlie to the boy next to him. The boy turned immediately from his book on powerful cars to look at the picture of the bleeding stump, ‘Ugh! Quicker than burning, or being hung, drawn and quartered though, ain’t it?’

Bryan stopped next to a girl, Maria, who had picked a book about cats and listened to her slowly pick through the words. She was way behind the others with her reading, but she tried her best and he gently corrected her pronunciation and helped her with the more difficult words.

‘Look at the pictures if you are not sure of the words. What’s the cat doing?’

Maria looked. ‘She’s licking the kittens.’

‘Good. So why is she doing that?’

‘To clean them up?’

‘That’s it. Good. So what do you think that word is, that’s linked with the mummy cat cleaning her kittens? It begins with ‘w.’’

‘Washing?’

‘That’s it! Good girl. The pictures help, don’t they?

Maria nodded, but looked unconvinced.

Latesha, Millie, Tracy, and another girl, Annie, were sniggering over a book. Bryan went across. They were reading, ‘*How we are born.*’

'What's going on here?'
'We don't understand this book,' said Latesha.
'What don't you understand?'
'Is a 'penis' a willy?' said Latesha. The others giggled.
Bryan felt uncomfortable. 'What does it say in the book, Latesha?'
'It says about a man's penis - and about it getting hard because he loves the woman in the picture, but I'm not sure if it's meant to be a willy, or something else?'
Bryan didn't believe her, and the other girls were clearly enjoying the conversation.
'Well, what else could it be?'
'I dunno,' she said in mock denial, but then burst into giggling laughter, the other girls joining in loudly with her.
'Alright, that's enough! I think you should choose another book, Latesha.'
She gazed at him, a fathomless expression on her face.

At three-thirty the children left the school in noisy groups to be greeted by their parents, grand-parents, or in some cases older siblings. A few fathers or grandfathers waited self-consciously, hoping they would be recognized by the others as bona fide guardians, and not prowling child molesters.
Bryan saw Tracy standing with Della.

‘Hello again,’ he greeted Della, ‘We don’t see you here normally, do we? Tracy usually goes back with the Harris twins, doesn’t she?’
‘That’s right. But I wanted to talk to you. You run on, Tracy.’
‘You’ll ask, won’t you mum?’
‘Go on!’ Tracy ran off.
Della looked at Bryan. ‘I’m a bit worried about her reading. She’s struggling with the books she’s supposed to be reading. I’m wanting a bit of extra tuition for her. I wondered if you’d be up for it?’

Bryan had had similar conversations with other mothers, and usually the question came in an embarrassed or shy way, as if they were asking him a personal question. But Della stared coolly at him as if confident of his answer. ‘The pay’s good,’ she added.
He felt the stir of desire for her again and was interested. ‘Can we talk about it?’ he said, ‘I need to check first what I’m doing for the rest of term.’ He was thinking how he might explain his absence from the house to Jennifer, and needed time to think of how this might be managed.
Della smiled at him. ‘Why don’t you come round after school? Where there’s a will, there’s a way, or so they say. We can talk about it; you can have some food, or whatever.’

Bryan hesitated; his late arrival back home after school hours would cause problems. However, on Saturday, Jennifer was due to take Adam to see her parents. Bryan would sometimes go too, but could absent himself if he had school work to prepare. Given the way things were at home right now, Jennifer wouldn't want him to go with her this week.
'I can come Saturday this week, about lunchtime,' he said.
She smiled. 'Come for lunch at twelve. Hope you've got a big appetite.'
**

On Friday evening, after Adam had been bathed and put to bed, Bryan and Jennifer pretended to watch television. Things were still not right between them. Bryan felt restless, excited, about seeing Della again. But this was mixed with doubt - and Jennifer's distance with him cranked up his guilty impatience and irritation toward her. The programme washed over them both, and he couldn't be bothered to discuss it or comment on it. They watched the late night news, their minds elsewhere, not taking in the economic crisis in the world, or the uprising in the Middle East. Her mind was in a whirl of annoyance with him and worry about work deadlines, compounded by the dragging weariness of childcare. His thoughts were on Della. They went to bed.

He lay looking at the pattern of lights on the bedroom ceiling from the passing cars. He just wanted to have sex with Della, that's all. And from the signs she had given him, that's all she wanted from him. That's what all men want, isn't it: uncomplicated sex; the subject of many loud, pissed conversations earlier in his life with men friends at college. He didn't want to move in with Della, or break up with Jennifer. He just wanted to shag her. Grab her black hair, stride her, and shag her.

The thought made him groan, and he turned to Jennifer. He reached out toward her, but he felt her body stiffen against him.

'I'm not in the mood; you've been horrible to me this last week.'

'I'm sorry…I'm sorry. Look, we need to make up. We can't go on like this.'

'It's all very well saying sorry, but I am getting overwhelmed with trying to look after Adam and do my work. You need to understand this, and help a bit more. You just don't care, do you? And…and you don't tell me you love me anymore.'

She felt close to tears again and turned on her side away from him.

He felt his irritation rise; he couldn't shake it away.

They lay in silence. His tiredness overtook him and he began to fall into a half sleep. Della was there, waiting. He jerked awake.

'I need you, Jennifer…please. Don't make me beg. We both need to. I love you…I love you!'

She reluctantly allowed him to touch and kiss her, but was numb and unresponsive. He knew this, understood why, and in the past he would have spent time kissing and stroking her until she relaxed. But tonight he did not; he did not want to. He mounted her and began to take her with a bucking, shuddering heat he had not experienced before.

Chapter Ten

December: The Feast of St. Rufus

The house was semi-detached, but with a side entrance beneath a flaking wooden canopy. It had once been council rented, but the crimson colour of the walls, and absence of privet hedge or regulation wooden fence at the front, marked it now as privately owned. The 'front garden' was no longer a garden, but a square of tarmac, stained with oil. The street was full of similar properties; most looked neglected. It was as if the initial burst of enthusiasm to buy a home had turned sour, and cynicism had set in after the first round of destruction and rebuilding had taken place.

The road was littered with cans, crisp packets, and the detritus from the nearby fast food shops. A group of teenagers lounged against the low railings of a small communal green area, its shrubs planted by the council earlier in the year now trampled underfoot. One lad had stepped away from the group and was booting a section of the railings, trying to batter them flat.

Bryan looked at the houses and felt a mixture of lust and aversion, with the latter quickly gaining ascendency. The house did not connect with the glamorous image of Della fixed in his mind. He had seen the area gradually decline and understood the wider economic problems: the lack of decent paid work and a dearth of jobs for the teenagers on the corner. But he was impatient with many of the residents for sinking alongside their estate, not clearing up the shit in the streets, not taking a pride in their houses, for getting drunk into a spewing, shouting oblivion every weekend, and for not pulling themselves up and doing something to improve their lives.

He had considered himself tuned in to their talk, their thinking - and at one level he was. But at a deeper level, he had turned away from them, mentally, socially, and emotionally, since he had returned to education, graduated, and moved into a professional career. But he was at Della's house. He thought of her at the disco, trying hard to revive the feelings that had propelled him here.

He loosened the top button of his open necked shirt and rang the bell. The door was opened almost immediately by Della, who had combed out her raven hair so it now fell around her shoulders. She was wearing a pink silk blouse and white three-quarter length trousers that emphasised her figure. She reached out to touch him lightly on his bare chest; a gold bracelet jingled on her wrist. 'Come in.'

He stepped inside, but felt his lust fast abating as he looked around. Della's expensive clothes clashed with the state of the house.
There was a patina of grease on the faded wall-paper, and the smell of fried food was masked by the prickling scent of lavender aerosol spray. A dog yapped in the rear garden.
They went into the front room. A huge black leather sofa dominated one side of the room, facing a wide screen television. A low table was laid with some shop-bought food alongside a bottle of sparkling white wine and two glasses.
On one wall there was a print, in lurid colours, of a naked woman, the front of her body pressed into the side of a white stallion, her arm cradling its head.
'Do you like it? Good, isn't it?'
He murmured his assent, but felt himself already recoiling and retreating from her, his instincts telling him he was in the wrong place. He noticed the dog hairs gathering in small heaps in the corners of the room, missed by the hurried sweeps of a vacuum cleaner that now stood in the corner, its lead trailing out behind.

He felt a sense of overwhelming panic and excused himself, ostensibly to use the toilet. At the top of the stairs the door of a bedroom was ajar. It was marked 'Tracy and Shelley.'

He began to see and realise the life Tracy led away from school. He pushed the door open and went in. The bunk beds were unmade; a grey duvet was strewn on the floor from the bottom bunk and lay amidst cotton-wool buds, unwashed clothes, and abandoned fashion magazines. The room smelt of cheap perfume, and a television was mounted on the wall opposite the bed. A computer was on a small table, its screen showing the Internet home page of a television celebrity.

'Wrong bedroom.' Bryan jumped in shock and turned to see Della in the doorway. 'Next door…come on. I'll show you my boudoir!'
He cringed at her tone, but followed Della into her bedroom. A double bed was spread with mauve silk sheets. Another print hung on the wall, this one of a naked couple standing in an embrace. The same stale smell from downstairs clung to the room. He stood frozen. He thought of his own home, the soft colours, the books, his wife and son.
Della sensed something was wrong and moved in close. 'You alright? A bit nervous? I like that. No need to be. Tracy and her sister are at my mum's house for the afternoon. It's just us two.'
He noticed the lines on her face now, concealed beneath the powder and cream. Her breath smelt of something fried. A panic rose again in his chest. What was he doing here? He had convinced himself that he was attracted to the open,

sensual frankness of women like Della. She had liked him, and had openly shown it; he was flattered, and was drawn to her.

But this was reality. Now. Here. With this woman, a single parent, with two stroppy pre-teen girls in tow.

He had lost all desire for her.

She saw the doubt and reached out one hand to pull his face to her, and the other to cup his balls.

He started back. 'No, I'm sorry… this is a mistake!'

She stared at him, as if struck, her face turning pale in its scorn and mounting anger as she read his mind.

'What the fuck are you doing here then?' Her spittle sprayed out flecking his shirt.

'I came to talk about Tracy,' he lied, feeling the need to get out of the house fast.

'You fucking liar! You knew what was what! What's your problem, eh? Can't do it with women?'

She stared at him as if discovering some truth. 'Maybe that's why you like to work with kids! You wanted to see if you could cut it with a woman, but you can't!'

He felt sick, disgusted with her, and with himself. 'I'm sorry, I've got to go.' He went to leave, but she blocked him.

'Yeah, that's it! I've got your number! You get your kicks from little girls, don't you?'

Her face was twisted with fury. 'You fucking perv… you bloody, middle-class poofter! So go, get the fuck out - and you keep away from our Tracy!'
He moved swiftly down the stairs and into the street, pursued by Della. She came to the door still shouting at him.
'You excuse for a man…can't get it up…piss off and don't come back!'
Neighbours had come to their doors to see what the commotion was about. She turned on them, 'What are you lot looking at?'
A voice shouted, 'You dirty tart!'
The teenagers on the corner sneered at him as he walked quickly away, her abuse stunning his ears.
**

Della sank into a chair and wept. She had thought she could have had something better with Bryan. Her husband, Mick, had cleared off to work on building sites in Germany two years ago, with no sign of him returning, and leaving her with the two girls. She thought of her struggle against loneliness and frustration at managing the two girls and a chaotic household. Mick sent her money every month, but how long would that last? Her supermarket job just paid a pittance. He had made one excuse after the other for not coming home, and she had now learned from a mate of his that he was renting a flat over there.

Why does life turn to shit? She and Mick had been good together at first. But that was before the kids came along. Then the rows started. She was landed doing all the work, while he stayed away more and more. He was either down the pub, or round his mum's house, and then he was offered a job in Germany. He didn't think twice about it. Off. Gone. The odd phone call from him - and that turned into a row every time. What's the betting that he'd be shacked up in the flat with some blond, fat-arsed German cow. Bryan had represented something better, different, a more intelligent relationship than with the apes, like Tony, that casually came and went through her life now.

She was not naïve enough to believe that Bryan would have wanted to be her live-in partner, but his regular presence in the home could have offered some form of stability; a good example for the girls, who were turning wild. He was a teacher, middle class - not in her usual sphere - but he didn't come over like the stuck-up ones she had met in the past. He was from around here too, spoke like around here, wasn't afraid to chill out at the disco. He looked like a regular man - or she thought he was. And she still had her figure, and knew how to please men. But she had seen the disgust in his face.

She was still sitting, smoking and nursing the half-empty bottle of wine, when Tracy returned.

'Why ain't he here? I thought you said he would still be here.'

'Well, he ain't, is he!' Della cried.

'What you done to scare him off?' Tracy shouted. 'Why can't we have him here, instead of that fat pig, Tony?'

Della stood up and grabbed her shoulders and shook her, 'Because we can't! That's why', she slurred, 'And why would he want to be around you? Bleeding noise… your shit and stuff all over the house. You never do anything to help me!'

Tracy sank on to the sofa and wept, 'I like him. He's nice to me. Dad's not coming home now. It's you…you've driven them both away now. I hate you!'

'What do you mean he's 'nice' to you? How is he nice to you? Has he touched you?'

'He likes me, I know, he's told me. He's interested in me… what I do…he asks me stuff…that's more than what you ever do. You don't care!' Her thin body shook as she sobbed.

'Has he touched you?' Della yelled, suspicion now mingling toxically with her anger.

Tracy sobbed, snot running down her face, 'What if he has? What would you care?'

**

Bryan opened the door of his house. He felt numb. The shame, mingled with fear of something unknown, unstoppable. He sank down and rocked on his haunches and buried his head into his arms.

'O Jesus! What have I done? What's the matter with me?'

After a while he pulled himself together and moved around the house, putting things away, tidying, cleaning, craving order, safety, normality. He touched his books, straightened the photos on the dresser of Jennifer and Adam; he found a Delius CD to play.

He sat and thought it through. Della would not want to take matters further with the school; it would make her look bad – a slut - if she did. He felt calmer.

When Jennifer and Adam returned the flat was clean, everything in place, food waiting for them, music in the background. He was attentive, listened to her about her day; asked about her parents. She was pleased, and thawed to him. She hated confrontation and saw his attention as his way of seeking reconciliation. Things were returning to normal for them again.

Chapter Eleven

Tracy had waited, growing increasingly impatient with Della. 'Have you heard if Dad is coming for tomorrow?' she asked for the fourth time that week.
Della contained her temper, 'I haven't heard from him. Look Tracy, he may just show up tomorrow, but don't bank on it. If he does, well that's good – for you. But if he doesn't, we'll have Christmas on our own. We had to last year, and it's likely to be the same this year. Don't build up your hopes on *him* anymore.'
'But I asked him on the phone, and he said he would.' Tracy had spoken to her dad a few weeks ago; a tearful conversation, as she poured out her grief and need of him.
'He said he might. That means, I'm afraid to say, he ain't!' Della was bitter at the memory of the last time she had spoken to him, his words casting a bleak verdict on her life and character.

'Why not? It's Christmas tomorrow. Why don't he come back just for Christmas?'
She missed her father. She missed his bulk, his smell, his rough, joking way with her. She missed the way he used to pick her up and swing her up on his broad shoulders and race up and down the garden, her squealing with delight.

‘We’ll make the best of it, whatever happens. I’ve got a joint, and we’ll have roast spuds, Yorkshires, the lot,’ said Della, making an effort to comfort her daughter, ‘and there’s that film on the telly in the afternoon.’

‘It ain’t the same without Dad!’

Della shrank from Tracy’s wails. She needed a drink now. She needed to make up, dress up, get out of the house, get pissed at the club - and see what else happened.

Tracy was awoken from a half sleep by the sound of her mother and another voice, male, ascending the stairs. Her spirits rose. It could be her father, come home in time for Christmas. The man’s heavy step echoed on the stairs, ‘Which one?’ he said.

‘Shh, keep your noise down, you’ll wake the kids.’

‘S’alright, they’ll think it’s Santa Claus!’ He broke into noisy, drunken laughter. Tracy didn’t recognize the voice. After a while loud, grunting noises came through the thin dividing wall.

‘Shelley, are you awake?’ The noise, though familiar to her from other men and other nights, frightened her. It was louder, more aggressive tonight.

‘They’re just bonking,’ said Shelley, ‘It’ll stop soon.’

Tracy had a rough idea what was happening, but was hazy on the finer detail. She asked cautiously, afraid of Shelley’s scorn, ‘That’s with his willy, ain’t it?’

Shelley jeered. 'What do you think, you spaz, it wouldn't be with his big toe, would it!'
Tracy was silent. Shelley knew she was afraid to ask her any more questions.
'You know what happens, don't you? The bloke shows he fancies you when his willy gets big, and he sticks it in the woman, you know where, don't you?'
Tracy suddenly realized she did know.

In the morning, Tracy, Shelley and Della sat at the kitchen table. Della had made a big effort to get up and lay the table for breakfast for them all. The man had not appeared, although they could hear him clumping around upstairs.
'I've got some presents for you later, after breakfast,' said Della. She had bought clothes, jewellery and music they could share.
But Tracy was still angry with her mother.
'Is he staying?'
'No, he ain't. And don't talk to me like that! For God's sake, let's get through today without another bleeding row!'
Heavy footsteps on the stairs announced the arrival of a large man in his forties with a shaven head.
'You want some breakfast?' said Della, not bothering to introduce him to her daughters.
'Naw. I'd better get back. They'll be expect…' He stopped.
'Yeah, they will won't they!'

He looked around at the hostile faces. ‘Come on girls. It’s Christmas. Where’s your presents then?’ he said, trying to jolly his way out of the house.
‘Why,’ said Della sarcastically, ‘have you got some for us then?’
‘You’ve had mine, girl, last night,’ he said, backing out, still trying to leave on a joke.
‘Yeah! Well it was smaller than you promised. And the batteries soon ran out!’
He glared at her. ‘Yeah, well go and fuck yourself!’
‘I might just as well have done! Now piss off!’
**

Bryan, Jennifer, and Adam sat together on the floor of their flat. They had had a late breakfast, and now opened presents together. He had chosen with care some jewellery for Jennifer, and had put together a leather album of family photos. She was pleased with these, and he felt normality and her love flooding back into his life. He had pushed the encounter with Della to the far corner of his mind. Adam grabbed and pulled at the bright paper and ripped open boxes. Soon toy cars, balls, crayons, spilled across the room. Bryan was happy. This was his life.
**

Jayne Boyle dreaded Christmas. She would take her mother to morning Mass, where happy family groups surrounded her on all sides: 'Happy Christmas! Happy Christmas!'

The priest would talk about love, and giving, and Christ's blessings. She would help her mother to the communion rail, and after Mass would wait behind her mother until those who came to greet her had drifted off.

Back home, she would give her mother some familiar and ritual presents – warm clothes, chocolates she liked, word puzzle magazines, two or three historical novels.

'I've read this one,' said Alice, but remembering it was Christmas added quickly, 'I'll read it again. I think I liked it.'

Alice would give Jayne an envelope with some money in it, accompanied with the inevitable, 'I couldn't get out to buy you anything. I wish I could.'

Jayne pushed back the thought she could have asked Iris, a friend who called in weekly to see Alice, to buy something for her.

The day now stretched endlessly ahead. A few relatives would telephone. Jayne would cook dinner, taking her time about it, and they would eat together in silence, Alice's thoughts hovering in the past, or wherever. They would watch the Queen's Christmas Broadcast, but then there was another seven hours before bed. Going for a walk on her own on Christmas Day would expose her loneliness to family groups trying out new bikes and scooters. Last year, in desperation, she had gone out clutching an empty parcel wrapped in tinsel and foil, and strode out briskly as if she were on her way to give a gift to someone special. But there was no one special, and she couldn't be bothered today with the self deception. She left her mother dozing in her chair and retreated to her room until it was time to make some supper for them both.

Chapter Twelve

January: The Feast of St. Agnes

It was a new term. Father Kelly was coming to Bryan's class today to lead the RE session. This happened at least once a term, and usually the children sat, glazed-eyed, while he spoke at them. But Father Kelly had been advised by the Diocesan Inspector to try something new: "try and engage the children more".
'A quiz,' he told Bryan in advance, 'Perhaps you could organise them into four teams, and we'll have an RE quiz.'

The children trooped along the corridor towards the classroom. Bryan stood at the door making sure they were all back; some children had been known to stay away from Father Kelly's sessions. He had smartened his appearance for the class. The last gaggle of children appeared: Maureen, Alice, and Tanya came along together talking in a friendly group. Maureen seemed happier these days and the other two girls were including her in their games at playtime. Tracy came last; on her own.
'You OK, Tracy? Anything wrong?'
Her eyes were wet. Her dad had not arrived for Christmas, and had not contacted them over the New Year period. She

couldn't find the words to say how she felt. She stood mutely in the corridor looking at him.
He was moved by her, and what he now knew of her life. He touched her shoulder, bent down to her and said quietly, 'OK, I can see you are upset. Whatever it is, you need to go in now. Father Kelly is waiting for us. We can talk about it later.'
She looked longingly at him.
**

Bryan had divided the class into four groups. Father Kelly explained the rules. 'All four groups start with ten points each. I'll ask each group a question; if they know the answer, and get it right, they get another five points. If they get it wrong, they lose five, and if they don't know the answer, I'll throw it open to the whole group. We'll see which group has the most points at the end. The group with the most points will be the winners. Is that all clear?'
The children nodded. They liked this type of thing.
'Is there a prize for the winning group?' asked a boy.
'I have some prayer cards for all the winners!' The children did well to conceal their disappointment, thought Bryan.
**

Bryan walked through the playground at break with Helen. 'Have you heard about your contract for next year?'

'Not yet,' said Helen, 'But I need the work for the part-time teaching certificate.' Helen had secured a place on a part-time course to train as a teacher, but needed the regular work practice to qualify.
'I'm sure you will be fine. You've done a great job so far.'
'I hope so. It would be great to get a permanent contract, but I'd settle for another temporary one.'
The sound of a child in pain rose distinctively above the normal playground sounds and Bryan and Helen turned toward it. A boy of six or seven had slipped and bruised his arm. He sat on the ground nursing it, wailing loudly, surrounded by other children who made no real effort to help him. Helen bent down beside him and established nothing was broken and that he wasn't bleeding. She rubbed it, and he stopped his wailing, but continued to grizzle.
'Do you want me to kiss it better?' she said, and planted a kiss on the bruised spot. The child immediately brightened, and the other children murmured their approval; this would be how most of their mothers would deal with the situation. Another boy, grabbing his chance, said 'I fell over and bruised my bum, Miss. Will you kiss it better?' All the children laughed.

Bryan and Helen continued around the playground and were approached by two older girls, who had broken away from a larger group.

'Come and see what we've done, Miss.' The girls had been practicing disco dance moves together. They walked over to the group. 'We've got it right now, Miss.'
'That's good.'
'Can we show you?'
Helen and Bryan looked at each other, she deferring to him.
'Come on then, let's see you all shake it,' said Bryan.
The girls went through a series of elaborate steps, forward, back, jump to the side, clap, jump in a half circle, and repeat.
Helen and Bryan clapped their approval.
The sound of the bell tolling the afternoon session ended the dance and the children trooped back inside the school.
**

Jayne Boyle made her way from the Head's office to Bryan Young's classroom. She struggled to conceal the warmth of the emotion she felt from showing in her face. The children were working quietly on arithmetic questions, but all looked up and abandoned their work when they saw the Deputy Head and the expression on her face.
'Bryan, go to the Head's office. I'll take over your class.'
He felt a sense of foreboding. She was stiffer than usual with him, and avoided eye contact.
'What's up?'
'The Head will explain. Will you go right away, please,' she said coldly.

At the office, the school administrators also avoided looking at him. 'Go right in.'

Bryan entered the head teacher's office. Thomas was there, with his office manager, Mary Brewer; a local representative from his teacher's union, Jim Osborne; and a woman he did not recognize. They all looked serious.
The Head introduced the woman, Katherine Andrews, an adviser from the local authority Human Resources department and explained that Mary Brewer was there to take notes of the meeting.
'Bryan, I've called a meeting because a serious allegation has been made against you – about inappropriate words and behaviour.'
He immediately thought of Della. 'Nothing happened. We didn't do anything together…' he said, and then stopped in confusion. Was this about Della - or something else?
They all looked at him sharply.
The Head continued, 'The allegation is that you kissed a child, Tracy Banks, and you told her you 'loved' her. When serious allegations are made against a teacher by a child or a parent we need to follow set procedures. I've been in touch with the local authority Lead Child Protection Officer, and acting on her advice the school will conduct an internal investigation, lead by Jayne Boyle. The results of the

investigation will be passed on to the Officer, and I will be liaising with her on the procedures to follow.'

Bryan listened, stunned, his thoughts in total confusion. He shook his head, 'This is…this is *ridiculous*! I've done no such thing.'
Thomas continued, 'I'm sorry Bryan, but acting on advice from the Officer, I am going to suspend you from teaching whilst this investigation is ongoing.'
Katherine Andrews said, 'You will be notified in writing of the reasons for this suspension and you will receive full pay during the investigation. If any other allegations come to light, you will also be advised of these.'
Thomas said, 'You should understand too, that other agencies may become involved, if it proves necessary.'
'Other agencies? Who do you mean?'
'Well, the police and social services could become involved. I need to take advice from the Child Protection Officer about this.'
Bryan stared at Thomas. He thought, 'Why in God's name would the police and social services be called in? What has Della been saying about me?'
Jim Osborne spoke for the first time. Bryan detected a touch of distaste in his voice. 'The Union will support you during the investigation. We can offer legal advice too, if it comes to it'

'Legal advice?'
'Yes…if it went to court, for example.'
Bryan felt light-headed; bile rose and scoured his throat.
Thomas said, 'I want to stress that the investigation will be fair and thorough, and you have been suspended to save you from the stress of having to work in school under these circumstances. If it is decided that there is no case to answer, you will be able to return to work and nothing will show on your records.'
'I must advise you, too,' continued Thomas, 'that during your suspension you must not discuss this with anyone in the school, as to do so could prejudice the inquiry against you. This is a confidential matter, and I don't want potential witnesses to be put under any pressure by you. This is in your interest, Bryan. Do you understand?'
Bryan nodded. His world was collapsing around him.
**

Jayne Boyle approached Helen in the staff room at the end of the day. 'Can I have a word outside, Helen?' Her tone indicated it would not be an informal matter. The other teachers stopped their conversations and listened. Something was wrong.
Bryan Young was missing, and someone had seen him cycling away from the school during the afternoon; Jayne Boyle had taken over his class.

The teacher who relieved Jayne Boyle later that afternoon reported that the children in Bryan's class were all subdued, sensitive to the sudden change of routine.

Jayne Boyle said, 'Don't look worried, Helen. This is not about you. And I'm sure you will be pleased to hear that your contract, along with your work review, is on the agenda to be discussed at the next Governor's meeting. This is about Bryan Young.'

'Bryan?'

'Yes. I want you to be discreet and not repeat our conversation to anyone. But I am investigating certain allegations against him.'

'What type of allegations?'

'Well, I am not at liberty to say what they are, only that they are serious, and involve allegations of…improper words and behaviour.'

'With the children here, at this school?'

'As I said, I'm not at liberty to say precisely. Let me ask you about Bryan. I noticed you with him today in the playground. What was happening with that group of girls?'

'They showed us some dance steps they had been practising.'

'How did this come about? I am concerned about who initiated this?'

'Well, I guess it was Bryan,' Helen said.

'Do you remember what he said?'

‘He said…”come on… let’s see you all…shake it”.’

‘Shake it. What do you think he meant?’

Helen shook her head; she felt as if the sides of the room were moving in toward her.

Jayne pursued her, her tone hardening. ‘Shake what? Do you think he meant for them to shake their bottoms?’

There was a brief silence. Jayne waited patiently, her eyes studying Helen. Helen said at last, ‘Yes, I suppose he did.’

Chapter Thirteen

'What this all about?' demanded Della. She had had a telephone call from the school asking her to go with Tracy to see Jayne Boyle. 'Come on! Tell me. What have you been up to?'

'Miss Boyle caught me drawing on the board.'

'Drawing on the board! What were you drawing?'

'A picture.'

'Tracy, I ain't gonna keep on asking you. What sort of bleeding picture?'

'Of Mr. Young and me.'

His name provoked a bitter response in her mind. 'Yeah, yeah! So what were you both doing in the picture?'

'He was kissing me.'

'Kissing you! What's this all about, Tracy?' Della shouted at her daughter, the humiliation of her rejection flooding back. 'Are you making up stories again? I'll bloody kill you if you are!'

She moved toward Tracy, who promptly burst into tears.

'He kissed me. He loves me…He told me he loves me.'

**

Jayne Boyle, Della and Tracy sat in an empty classroom. Jayne put a small tape-recorder in front of her and showed them a photo she had taken of the white-board drawing. The erect penis mocked Della.

Jayne said, ‘I’ve spoken to you about this already, but I want to ask you again, Tracy, with your mother here, and I want you to think very carefully before you speak. And I want you to tell the truth and shame the Devil, Tracy. Will you do that?’

Tracy nodded.

‘Who is the man in the picture supposed to be?’

‘Mr. Young.’

‘Mr. Young, are you sure about that?’

Tracy nodded.

‘What is he supposed to be doing in the picture?’

‘He’s kissing me.’

‘Is this something that has happened, or something you’ve imagined? Now think carefully about this, Tracy.’

Tracy hesitated. ‘It happened. He loves me, he said he loves me.’

Della felt her stomach tighten.

‘When did he kiss you? Jayne asked.

‘On Tuesday morning.’

‘So two days ago; this week?’

‘Yes.’

‘When did he say that he loved you?’

‘At the same time.’

'So you say Mr. Young kissed you and said that he loved you, and this happened two days ago. What time was this, and where did this happen?

'I dunno the exact time.'

'Before or after the morning break?'

'After.'

'What class did you go to next?'

'Father Kelly – he had a quiz.'

'Did anyone see you and Mr. Young?'

'No, we were in the corridor; he did it in the corridor. All the others had gone into class.'

'Where did he kiss you – on what part of your body?'

'On my neck.'

'And what exactly did he say to you when you say he kissed you?'

'He said I was his favourite, and he liked to talk to me - and that he loved me.'

'Now Tracy. Tell me why you have drawn this? Jayne pointed to the phallus.

'I dunno.'

'Well, tell me what it is supposed to be.'

'It's Mr. Young's willy .'

'Why have you drawn it like this?'

'Because men's willies get hard when they like someone.'

'So are you saying that Mr. Young's …willy… was hard when he was in the corridor?'

'Yes.'

'Tracy, how do you know it was hard?'

'I saw it.'

'He showed it to you?'

'Well I saw it. You can ask Latesha and Millie too, they know about it, and I drawed it for them.'

'Thank you, Tracy, I will. But are you saying it was out in the open, exposed to you when he was in the corridor?'

'No, but I could see it was hard through his jeans.'

'Did he say anything about it being hard?'

'No, but he loves me, and I knew it was; I could see it was.'

'Alright Tracy, now tell me more about Mr. Young and exactly what he means to you?'

'He's nice to me. He's kind. He listens to me. I love him, and he loves me. I could have had him as a private teacher, but mum messed things up with him.' Tracy broke into loud sobbing tears.

Jayne waited until the child stopped crying. 'Wait outside, Tracy, while I talk to your mother.'

Tracy left. Jayne felt her dislike of Della rise. 'What did Tracy mean about having Mr. Young as a private teacher?

'Well, he saw me after school, when I was waiting for Tracy, and told me she wasn't doing too well with her reading.'

'Yes? So?'

‘He offered to give her some extra tuition. I asked him to come to the house to discuss it, as I weren’t sure about it. He came to the house, but I kicked him out.’
‘You asked him to leave. Why?’
‘I caught him upstairs snooping around in Tracy and Shelley’s bedroom. I was suspicious of him. And I found out that Tracy has got him on her camera and put pictures of him all over the Internet. You can see it yourself if you do a search. I thought it was all innocent, but I can see what he was up to now. He even said that Tracy was sexy, to my face!’

Della had worked herself up to a fury of indignation. This explained his behaviour, she rationalized. He was a bloody pervert, a pansy, a nonce, just like all the bloody priests in the news. What was it with these supposed do-gooder Catholic blokes?
‘When did Mr. Young say that Tracy was ‘sexy’?’
‘It was after the disco. As I say, I didn’t think anything of it at the time, but I can see his dirty game now.’
‘Why didn’t you let the Head know about this, Mrs. Banks?’ Jayne asked.
‘I didn’t think you would do anything about it. To be perfectly honest, I thought you would just cover it up, just like all the stuff that’s been happening with priests lately.’
**

Jayne sat with Latesha and Millie and their mothers, and with her tape recorder in front of her.

'Neither of you are in trouble about anything, so don't worry, and I am going to ask some of your classmates the same questions I'm going to ask you. Are you happy with me doing that?'

Both girls nodded.

'If you can't answer a question, that's fine, it's not a problem, but I want you both to answer truthfully. Do you understand that?'

The girls began to look more apprehensive, but nodded their understanding.

'Are you happy about me taking a recording of what we say? When I write down later what you said, I want to make sure I have got it right. Is that alright with you?'

They nodded.

'OK, let's start. Are you both happy here at school?'

Latesha said, 'yes,' and Millie nodded.

'Are the teachers nice to you?'

Millie looked at Latesha, who said, 'They're alright.'

Latesha's mother intervened, 'You told me you liked all of them.'

'They're alright,' Latesha repeated sullenly.

Jayne said, 'Tell me who your class teacher is this year?'

Latesha said, 'Mr. Young.'

'How do you get on with Mr. Young?'

Latesha sensed he was at the heart of this questioning, and that he was in some sort of trouble, probably over Tracy's drawing on the whiteboard. 'I don't like him as much as some of the others,' she said.
'This is the first I've heard of it,' said her mother.
Jayne quickly intervened. 'Can you tell me why that is, Latesha?'
'He picks on us, don't he, Millie?' Millie nodded. 'And he has touched me. He shouldn't do that, should he? And he touches other children too.'
Jayne felt as if she was closing in on her prey. 'Will you be able to give me the names of other children you say Mr. Young touches?' Latesha nodded. She mentioned some names, including Tom and Maureen.
'You say that he picks on you, and has touched you, tell me in what way; give me an example?'
'He pushed me in a corner and grabbed my arms and said I was to look at him because I was making it hard for him.'
Jayne glanced across at Latesha's mother, who looked as if she was going to interrupt again. Jayne quickly said, 'What do you think he meant by 'making it hard for him'?'
'I suppose it was about his willy getting hard. That's what he wanted me to look at, weren't it, Millie, you thought that too, didn't you?' Millie nodded her agreement.
Millie's mother, who hadn't spoken either, just stared in shock at her daughter and shook her head.

'How do you know about these things, Latesha … about men's bodies?' asked Jayne.
'Mr. Young brought a book into the class for the bookshelf, with pictures of men and women with nothing on, and he has talked to me, Millie, and Tracy about it.'
'Annie was there, too,' said Millie.
'You say he talked to you about it. What did he say exactly?'
'I don't remember exactly,' said Latesha, 'But it was about men's willies.'
Her mother said, 'Are you sure about this, Latesha. You're not making this up? This is serious you know, it's not a game!'
'Yeah! I'm sure. I was there, weren't I. So were Tracy, Annie and Millie. They saw the book and heard him too.'
Jayne said, 'Did Mr. Young give you the book to look at in the class?'
Latesha hesitated. 'The book was on the table when we got there. We picked it up and started to read it.'
**

Tom and his mother sat across from Jayne Boyle. She explained again that she was making some enquiries about allegations that other children had made about a teacher, and that Tom was not in any trouble.
'Do you like this school, Tom?'

Tom said he did. His mother confirmed that he enjoyed coming to school.
'Are the teachers nice to you?' Jayne asked.
'Yes,' he said.
'All of them?'
'Yes, they're all nice to me.'
'Do any of the teachers have physical contact - touch you - in any way during classes or in the playground?' Jayne asked.
Tom's mother immediately looked worried. 'Is this what this is about? Tom, answer Miss Boyle'
Tom shook his head, his eyes filled with tears.
'Tom, you're not in any trouble,' said Jayne Boyle, 'Don't be afraid to say.'
'Miss Weir touched me on the head and said I was good at RE. But I didn't mind her doing it. She won't get into trouble, will she?'
'No, no, don't worry, she won't. Has any other teacher done anything else like this?'
He shook his head. 'I can't remember.'
'Let me give you names of other teachers. If any of them has touched you, you can just say 'yes.' You don't mind doing that, do you?' He said he didn't mind.
Jayne read out a list of names of women teachers. Tom shook his head, although at one name he said, 'I think she

patted me on the arm once when I read to her and said I was a good reader.'

Jayne said Bryan's name. Tom nodded.

'Tell me about Mr. Young,' said Jayne.

'I was reading to him recently, and he put his hand on my shoulder,' said Tom.

'Do you know why he did that?'

'I can't remember, but I didn't mind.'

'Did he do anything with his hand?'

Tom frowned in concentration. 'I can't remember … no, I don't think so.'

'Did he just put his hand on your shoulder, or rub it up and down?'

'I don't remember, he just put it there, I think,' Tom said, anxiously.

His mother said, 'Is this about, Mr. Young?'

'I can't say any more at this stage,' said Jayne.

'I can't believe Mr. Young would do anything wrong. Tom likes him, and he has helped him a lot with his reading.' Isn't that right, Tom?'

'Yes, I like him. He's nice to me.'

'Nice', said Jayne. 'Can you give me an example of ways he is nice to you?'

Tom thought. 'He's a laugh, he tells us jokes. But he's quite strict too…and he makes the lessons fun.'

**

Maureen and her mother sat in the office, both looked defeated by life. Maureen's mother was a woman in her late thirties, but she looked older. She was shabbily dressed and her hair hung limply around her face. She clutched a plastic handbag tightly and sat on the edge of her seat, avoiding eye contact with Jayne.

'Thank you, Mrs. O'Hara, for bringing Maureen along today. I want to reassure you both that there is no allegation against you, Maureen. You have done nothing wrong at all. I just want to ask you some questions about a teacher in this school, and I have to ask these questions to find out if the teacher has acted properly or not. Do you understand that?'

Maureen nodded at Jayne.

'Alright, Maureen, I want to ask if any of the teachers has had physical contact with you – by that, I mean has touched you?'

Mrs. O'Hara looked up in alarm and turned towards her daughter, who had turned red with embarrassment.

'Touching! O Blessed Mary! Not that! Not in this school!'

Jayne quickly intervened. 'There may be nothing to worry about at all. I just want to establish if any teacher is more likely than the others to touch the children – and not necessarily in a way to cause you alarm, Mrs. O'Hara - but just in general. For example, did I not see Mr. Young holding your hand in the playground recently?'

Maureen nodded.

'Tell me about that. Why was he holding your hand?'

Maureen told Jayne about the incident in the classroom and how Bryan had helped her to find Alice to play with.

'What was Mr. Young saying to you?'

'I don't remember. Nice things.'

'What sort of nice things?'

Maureen thought hard. 'I don't remember exactly, but I liked him talking to me… I think he said about the disco, and how he hoped I would come to it with my mum.'

Chapter Fourteen

Thomas, Jayne Boyle, Father Kelly, and a woman, formally dressed, in her late forties sat together. Thomas introduced Mary Edwards, Lead Child Protection Officer for the local education authority, to the others.

'I would like us to review the information Jayne has collected so far to see where we go from here with this. Mary will advise us on the next steps. Jayne, will you summarise what you have learned so far, please.'

Jayne consulted her notes. 'Just to remind you, the allegation against Bryan Young came to light when I saw Tracy Banks drawing on the whiteboard in 3B.'

She paused to show them the photograph she had taken.

'Tracy claims it represents Bryan Young kissing her. She claims he has told her that he loves her, and that he kissed her, last week, Tuesday, in the corridor; this would be around eleven.'

Jayne continued, 'I have asked her about the sexual nature of the drawing and she claims that Bryan was…sexually excited when he was kissing her, and that she could see his erect penis through his jeans.'

Father Kelly shook his head, 'Dear, dear, dear!'

'Tracy claimed that Bryan has discussed male sexual arousal with other pupils, and she named Latesha Harris and Millie Hughes as witnesses. I spoke to both these girls in the presence of their parents, and Latesha and Millie both claim that this happened during a recent reading session in Bryan's class.'

Jayne again consulted her notes. 'Annie Morris was in the group too, but she seems vague about what happened, and said she wasn't really listening, although she remembers a book that the others were looking at when she joined them. It was the 'How we are born' book that gave us some problems a while ago.' She looked across at Father Kelly and Thomas.

Father Kelly said, 'Yes, this is the one we objected to, wasn't it? Bryan's choice, I remember.'

Thomas nodded, 'It was.'

Jayne continued, 'I have spoken to other pupils'; she named those she had interviewed so far. 'Bryan appears to be inclined to touch pupils – not in an overtly sexual way, so far – but by, for example, putting his arm on a boy's shoulders, holding hands with a girl, that sort of thing. He also has encouraged the girls to dance for him in the playground.'

She mentioned her discussion with Helen. 'Helen tells me that Bryan said to a group of girls, "Let's see you all shake it". I asked her about 'shake it,' and Helen believed he meant for them to shake their bottoms.'

Jayne continued, 'He has also been filmed dancing among a group of girls in the playground.'

Thomas stared at her, 'Filmed!'

'Yes, Tracy Banks filmed him dancing with the girls in our playground and, I'm afraid, it gets worse, she has put this onto a social network Internet site for all the world to see - with a commentary about 'my cool, cool teacher.' I found it quite easily by doing a search. I have to tell you, too, I'm sorry, Father, but you were the butt of the children's cruel jokes in the film - about your weight - and Bryan appeared to ignore the comment; he certainly didn't reprimand the child involved. There's also a photo of him too, on the same website, standing close to Tracy's mother, Mrs. Della Banks, taken straight after the disco, or so it seems. They look quite…close, if not intimate. But you can judge this for yourself.'

'I think we need to look at this straight after your briefing, Jayne,' said Thomas. The others nodded. Father Kelly was silent.

'With regards to Mrs. Banks, she claims that Bryan approached her to talk about Tracy's progress and offered her daughter extra tuition after school hours. I understand that he has not approached the Head for permission to do this.'

Thomas confirmed it was school policy that all such initiatives should be agreed with the senior management of the school, and usually discussed at a Governor's Meeting, but this had not happened.

Jayne continued, 'Mrs. Banks alleges that Bryan visited her one Saturday morning to discuss this extra teaching with her, but while he was there he made an excuse and went upstairs. She said she was suspicious, followed him up, and found him in Tracy's bedroom. He didn't have any reason for being there, and so she asked him to leave.'

At this point Mary Edwards, who had been making notes, intervened, 'What did she say about this incident exactly?'
'Mrs. Banks used the word 'snooping' about his presence in her daughter's room, and said that she became very suspicious about his motives.'
'Why didn't she report it to the School?' asked Thomas.
Jayne repeated what Della had said to her.
Father Kelly responded with heat. 'Yes, this is the trouble now! We're all branded with the same dirty brush. This is why we need to take clear action in this case.'
'I understand your frustration, Patrick,' said Thomas, 'But we are still in the enquiry stage and we need to be seen to be fair to all involved. Anything else, Jayne?'
'Only that Tracy Banks seems infatuated with Bryan and, I think, putting aside the specific kissing allegation for the moment, the issue for me is to what extent has he encouraged all this? We saw Tracy's behaviour towards him for ourselves at the disco. And from talking to the children, and from my own observations, he seems to project himself

to the children as rather an anti-establishment figure; a bit of a 'I'm on your side,' sort of thing. Of course, we want the children to enjoy school and to like their teachers, but we all know, sadly, of teachers who need the company of children to meet their own needs, rather than to meet the needs of the children.'

Jayne caught the eye of Mary Edwards, who nodded in agreement, as she had said the same thing in an article published recently in the education press.

Thomas said, 'Mary, I would appreciate your observations so far and some advice on our options in dealing with this matter.'

Mary Edwards took her time in responding. 'Thank you, Headmaster. I think what we may have here is a pattern of behaviour that we can associate with sex offending, and in particular the grooming of children by adults for their sexual gratification.'

She paused to allow her words to sink home.

'From experience, and from studying this subject extensively over the last twenty years, sex offenders in positions of trust in schools are often viewed by their colleagues, and the children, as rather non-conformist in their actions and appearance. I was, therefore, interested in your summary, Jayne, on Mr. Young's attitudes.' The two women exchanged quiet smiles.

‘This is a way of establishing rapport with the children for their own ends,’ she continued, ‘Other ways include joking, banter, that sort of thing: anything that reduces the necessary social distance there should be between pupil and teacher.’
Thomas, Jayne and Father Kelly all nodded in agreement.
‘The sex offender then starts to identify the more vulnerable children; children that he, and it is invariably a man, recognizes as more trusting or open to his advances. These advances come cautiously at first: by gentle touching, on the shoulder, arm or back, or holding the child’s hand, and giving the child expressions of individual concern, often in secretive ways – by whispering in their ear, for example. This can move on to more overt sexual behaviour, by kissing the child, or touching the child’s body in more intimate places, and by encouraging the child to witness and, eventually, fondle his own body.’

She stopped for a moment. There was complete silence in the room.
‘Serious concerns for me are the allegation by Tracy: about the kissing in the corridor, and the visit by Mr. Young to the house, where he is caught by the mother in the girl’s bedroom. Building up a relationship of trust with a child’s family is a classic way that sex offenders operate, as they work to become seen and recognized as a person that a child can be safe with.’ She paused and looked at them.

Thomas broke the silence, 'So where do we take this now, Mary?'
'Well, in some cases of this nature, where there is a high degree of ambiguity in what was said, or went on, a Head could decide to deal with the matter internally by, for example, issuing a written or verbal warning or caution.' Her tone indicated, however, that this should not be an option. 'But we need to keep in mind that there have been twenty sexual abuse cases involving teachers or teaching assistants in the district over the past year, and this is a particularly sensitive issue in some faith schools at this time.' She glanced at Father Kelly, who quickly nodded in agreement.
'I suggest the school needs to take strong action. In a case like this, procedures dictate that the police are informed so they can look into Mr. Young's background and check out his home circumstances. What do we know about these?'
'We think he is in a relationship with a woman, and there may even be a child in the household,' said Jayne.
'If there is, social services will need to be involved to ensure the child is not at risk. I would suggest too, that the school appoints an external investigator to work alongside you, Jayne, to take the pressure off you, and to collect additional statements from witnesses, and to interview Mr. Young.
I don't think it wise that a member of staff interviews him; the school needs to be seen to be behaving impartially

toward him, and he may feel that a senior member of staff may have an axe or two to grind. I have a private sector company in mind that is experienced in these cases. One of their investigators would interview him and conduct additional interviews with key witnesses to clarify points and to test statements made earlier to you, Jayne.'

Thomas said, 'I would have to take this to a Governor's Meeting because of the cost implications – I imagine we are talking several thousands of pounds for this service?'

Mary agreed that it would.

Father Kelly said, 'Would a child sex abuser fit such a profile as Bryan Young's? I mean, if he has a wife, or partner, and children?'

'Yes. Abusers can come from every class, profession, and background. As I mentioned earlier, most offenders are men and many of them are in relationships with women and have children of their own, or are living with step-children. Many of them have been the victims of abuse themselves when they were children. That's something the police will look at.'

Thomas said, 'Thank you, Mary. I think we need to take your advice completely in this matter'; the others nodded and murmured their agreement. 'I can't imagine what Bryan Young will have to say about all this. But one line of argument might be that the children are making this all up, particularly Tracy Banks.'

Mary smiled. 'Of course, individual children can fantasize. But what we have here are a number of incidents and behaviours that form a clear pattern. We must ask ourselves too, why should children make up stories of this nature? In the past, as we now know to our cost, children were not believed. And who could believe that teachers - or priests – could behave in these awful ways? But, sadly, we know that they do. And we must ask ourselves, when faced with this type of allegation, is it a one-off incident, capable of misinterpretation, or is it a link in a chain of related incidents that have come, or are coming to light?'

She continued. 'We have to ask ourselves too, is there the ring of truth about what the children say – no matter how uncomfortable that makes us feel? In cases like this, even if the police decide to take no action - because the burden of proof is not strong enough for a criminal conviction - an internal disciplinary hearing can look at things differently. The internal hearing, involving the school Governors, can look at 'balance of probabilities,' meaning that, in all probability, the allegations are true ones.'
'Will the children have to attend the disciplinary hearing?' asked Thomas.
'No. And that's why we need to gather written evidence in statements from the children. That's where the investigator

can help; it's a time-consuming process. But I would like to thank Jayne for the painstaking work she has done so far.'

There was a murmur of assent; they all nodded their appreciation at Jayne.

Chapter Fifteen

January: The Feast of Saint Flavian

'I am in hell,' thought Bryan.
'This is complete madness,' he said aloud. Jennifer started from her own depression and stared at him. It broke the silence in the room. He had come home from school over a week ago now and told her the news. He told her what they had told him: about allegations of kissing Tracy Banks and telling her he loved her, and that the school were making enquiries on 'related matters.' He sensed that the incident with Della was connected with this in some way, and this preyed on his mind day and night; but he could not summon the courage to tell Jennifer what had happened.

She had quizzed him incessantly about why Tracy should say such a thing, and at first he had no idea, but then he remembered the writing lesson, the sessions in the playground - and her hanging on to his arm at the disco. The only guilt he felt was related to Della, but he clung to the hope that she would not want to say anything about this – but the fear remained that she might have made up some other allegation to strike back at him.

During the day he now looked after Adam, giving Jennifer more time to work, but Bryan's constant agitation and frustration at this change of routine was sensed by the boy, who constantly whined after his mother, pursuing her to her study whenever he could escape from Bryan. This wound Jennifer up even more and led to shouting matches between them. She could not believe him capable of behaving in this way to a girl in his class, but an allegation had been made, so a doubt had been planted in her mind. She brooded: do we ever know someone? What goes on in someone's mind? Was Bryan capable of operating at different levels: loving and normal with us, but with a part of his personality buried and unknown, until now?

The police came: two plain clothes constables from the local Child Protection Section, a man and a woman, both in their mid thirties. They were outwardly polite, but both looked coolly at him, a faint whiff of disdain in the air. Bryan was relieved that Jennifer and Adam were out when they had telephoned to make an appointment, and he had opted to see them on his own.

The male officer, David Nicholls, cautioned him: 'You do not have to say anything, but it may harm your defence if you do not mention when questioned something which you later rely on in court. Anything you do say maybe given in evidence. Do you understand?'

The woman, Paula Whitehead, took notes.

'Yes'.

The officer relaxed his tone a little. 'You are not under arrest, Mr. Young, and you have the right to legal advice at any time.'

Bryan nodded, 'I haven't got anything to hide.'

The officers took details of his history and circumstances. They asked to see photos of Jennifer and Adam. They were concerned about the kissing allegation – and the fact that he was appearing on Tracy Bank's social network site on the Internet. He paled. This was the first he knew about this. Did he have a computer himself? He did, and they politely but firmly asked to take it with them to check its hard drive.

'Check for what?'

Pauline Whitehead replied. Well, the main thing is that we will be searching for pornographic or other suspicious or compromising images…of children. We will also be searching for e-mail messages between you and children at the school, or elsewhere. Will we find any?'

'No, no…no! Of course not!' Bryan felt relieved, as there were nothing to find, but was horrified they thought there might be.

David Nicholls, said, 'I understand that you visited Tracy's house. Is that correct?'

Bryan immediately felt guilty. 'Yes. I went there at Tracy's mother's invitation?'

The two officers looked briefly at each other.

Nicholls continued, 'Well, there is some dispute about that. But our main interest in this is in that you were asked to leave the house after being found by Mrs. Banks in Tracy's bedroom. Is that correct?'

'Yes.'

'Why were you in Tracy's bedroom?'

He decided to just state the truth in this. 'I had been asked to tutor Tracy. She is a girl with problems at school: attention seeking, a little disruptive, that sort of low-level thing. When I went to the house, and saw where she lived, I began to get an idea about the reasons for her behaviour. I went into her bedroom for the same reason - to see how she lived - the influences on her life. That was the reason, no other, but I realise how stupid it was now.'

'So why did Tracy's mother throw you out of the house?'

The detective consulted his notebook. 'She told the school she found you, in her words, 'snooping' about in there. Surely if you had said the same to her as you said to me, she would not have reacted in this way?'

Bryan wrestled with the urge to tell them what had happened at the house, but fear of the consequences with Jennifer gripped him.

He shook his head. 'She didn't give me the chance. She must have jumped to the wrong conclusion. But I swear to God I had no evil intention toward that girl, or any other child!'

The stress of the last week swept over him and he wept, the sorrow, anger, and guilt pouring out in an uncontrollable stream.

Pauline Whitehead approached and touched him lightly on the shoulder. 'Look, Mr. Young. We know that you have no previous convictions or police cautions for improper behaviour with children. If there is nothing on your computer, well, I can't speak for my senior colleagues and the Crown Prosecution Service, as it's their decision on this matter, but if there is no incriminating evidence found, and no more possible criminal allegations made by other children at the school, then…' She hesitated, knowing that she was giving too much information away, '…then you are perhaps over-stressing yourself now about the consequences of our visit, although I do understand your feelings.'

Her experience and instincts told her that, whatever else this man had done, a prosecution would not succeed; the evidence was too thin.

The police removed the computer and left. Bryan sat holding the receipt they had given him, the paper shaking in his hands. He suddenly realized that Jennifer's current work project was on the hard drive. He did not know if she had made a copy. When Jennifer returned, he explained what had happened. She had not made a copy, and was behind with the project. It would not now be finished in time. They sat, silent, beyond words, staring at the walls.

The following day two social workers telephoned and asked for an appointment to meet them both and to see Adam. The two women were, like the police officers, polite, but conveyed a sense of forensic detachment to their task. They explained that, as a serious allegation had been made concerning children, their job was to ensure that Adam was in no danger. The older woman, Verity Hughes, asked most of the questions whilst the younger, Nicola Parsons, took notes of the conversation and quietly looked around, mentally noting the contents and order of the house.

'How would you describe your relationship with each other?' Verity asked, looking at both of them to see who would reply.

'Good… it has been good,' said Bryan.

'Has been?'

He bridled. 'It still *is* good!'

'Is that right, Jennifer?'

'Look, we are a normal couple. I love Bryan, we both love Adam, and I'm horrified by these allegations. We both are.

I'm sickened by the suggestion that I would allow anyone…Bryan…or anyone to hurt Adam.'
'There is no such suggestion,' Verity replied smoothly. 'But we need to make sure he is safe. You want that; so do we.'

Jennifer breathed rapidly, trying to contain herself. The thought that others believed Bryan might harm Adam strengthened her defensive feelings toward him.
Bryan was simply not the type of person to abuse children. This feeling sank deep and touched a bedrock of love she felt for him. Call it instinct, faith, love, anything, but whatever else he might do, child abuse was not in his nature. She knew this.
'I know Bryan. We have known each other for over ten years. I know, I just know, he would not do the things he has been accused of. I trust him with Adam. I really do. This thing is a total nightmare.'

She looked toward the next room where, through the open door, she could see Adam playing. They all went to talk to the boy. Adam beamed at the sudden attention, and the two social workers visibly slipped from their official personas to being animated, warm and childlike with him. He tottered around the room happily, bringing toys for their inspection.
Later, as Nicola engaged Bryan with form filling, Verity took Jennifer to one side. 'Jennifer. If there is anything you

want to say to us in confidence – about Bryan. Then you can make an appointment to see me.' She gave Jennifer a telephone number.

'No, no, no! There's nothing else I want to say.'

'Well… just remember, you can. There's no need to be afraid.'

'I'm not!'

Verity looked at her for a few seconds without speaking.

'We will need to call again over the next few weeks.'

'When? And why? Aren't you satisfied with what you've seen today?'

'I can't say when we will call. As to why, well, we are acting in everyone's best interests, Jennifer, particularly Adam's. I'm sure you will appreciate this in time.'

Chapter Sixteen

Thomas had called a special Governor's Meeting to let them know about the allegations and to get their agreement to appoint an external investigator. Derek Hartley, Harry Bowen, Ali Desai, Margaret Rogers, and two other parent governors: Peter Foster; and another woman, Elli Curtis, had gathered. They were all curious as to the cause of the meeting.

Without going into all the detail, Thomas explained that Bryan Young had been accused of 'inappropriate words and behaviour' with a number of girls in his class and had been suspended to allow the allegations to be investigated. There would be an internal disciplinary hearing and a number of the Governors would be appointed to listen to the evidence and reach a decision. If Bryan should be found guilty and consequently dismissed, he would have the right of appeal.

They listened in silence until Thomas had finished.

Derek Hartley spoke hesitatingly, 'By 'inappropriate,' do you mean of… of a sexual nature?'

Thomas said, 'I can't go into too much detail, but yes, I'm afraid so.'

'This is all very shocking… shocking,' said Ali Desai.

'Who are the children involved?' asked Elli.

'As I say, I can't go into specifics yet. The police are investigating, and social services have been informed, as Mr.

Young is living with 'a partner,' and a young child; his son, apparently.'

'Have the press got onto this yet?' said Derek Hartley.

Thomas shook his head, 'No, and it is important we all maintain confidentiality about this matter. We don't want the school to be tainted by this type of allegation.'

Derek Hartley agreed. 'Yes, I agree, it could affect my business too, if it came out I was Chair of Governors at the school. The press would be onto me for comment, and I don't want that sort of publicity.'

Peter Foster nodded in agreement, 'Yes, we'll all be tarred with the same brush. It will be a case of "those Catholics are at in again", type of ignorant response.'

'But the matter is still being investigated, isn't that right?' Margaret Rogers asked quietly, 'So we don't know if the allegation against Mr. Young is true or not?'

Thomas slightly resented the implication in her voice. 'Yes. Yes. That's quite right, Margaret. Bryan Young is still under investigation - which brings me to the question of money.'

He explained about the need to appoint an external investigator to interview Bryan. 'It's important for the school to be seen as scrupulously impartial in this, particularly when Bryan Young is confronted with the specifics of the allegations. We don't want him making counter-accusations against senior staff, about 'getting back at him,' or similar comments.'

‘Would he have any reason to make that sort of allegation against you or other colleagues?’ asked Margaret.
‘No. Not at all, but we need to think of all possible eventualities,’ said Thomas quickly.
‘Yes, quite right, I agree. I was in the Forces and I’ve seen this happen when men are charged with disciplinary offences,’ said Derek Hartley.
‘Would you be willing to be chair of the Disciplinary Hearing, Derek?’ asked Thomas.
Derek agreed that he would; he was pleased he had been asked.
**

Thomas entered Bryan’s classroom. The children were subdued and looked at him warily. Jayne Boyle, and supply teachers, had been teaching Bryan’s class since his suspension, but Thomas had decided to teach the class himself today when one of the cover teachers had phoned in sick.
He also wanted to start to impose a firmer hand on the children, who some of the teachers, including Jayne Boyle, had found to be surly and uncooperative since Bryan’s absence.
‘Good morning children.’
‘Good-morning-Mister-Wood.’

‘I don’t think I saw and heard everyone wishing me a good morning. That wasn’t very polite, was it?’

The children shuffled in their seats; Thomas noted some scowls from a few boys, Charlie Morton among them. He remembered Charlie from the last time he was here.

‘So, let’s start again shall we.’ It was not a request.

‘Good morning children.’

‘Good morning Mister Wood.’ The children were louder, but slower in their response, as if grudging him the words.

It was an English class, but with the Diocesan Report in mind, Thomas wanted to link the reading to a religious education lesson.

A monitor from each group gave out the set book.

‘Let us all read from ‘The Life of Jesus’. Turn to page 6. This picks up on the story of Our Blessed Lord’s life following his birth - which was where?’

The children dropped their eyes.

‘Which was where?’ He repeated, raising his voice.

‘Maureen?’

Maureen went scarlet. ‘Bethlehem’, she said to the desk-lid.

He looked around at the closed faces, and felt his temper rising.

‘This is what happens when children are encouraged to treat every lesson as a game’, he thought, ‘sullenness and resentment, when another stricter teacher has to replace a Pantomime Fool.’

'Alright. I'm going to start, but I will select children at random to continue, so give the story your full attention.'

'Now King Herod, who ruled Judea, was told of the visit of the Wise Men to his kingdom, so he sent a message for them to visit him.'
Thomas read, but at the same time scanned the faces of the children to see who was not paying attention.
'The Wise Men told Herod it was prophesied that a child would be born at that time to become King of the Jews and they had followed a guiding star from afar to Herod's Kingdom. Now King Herod was a vain and jealous man and was angry at this news. But, quietly and smiling, he said slyly to the Wise Men: 'Go and search for the child and when ye have found him, bring me word again, that I may come and worship him also.' And the Wise Men departed, and lo, the Star went again before them until it came to the place where the Child Christ was sleeping.'
The children's faces were bent low toward their books. Thomas stopped and scanned the tops of their heads.
'Do we have a volunteer to continue the story?'
The room was quiet.
'Come along now. It is an easy enough story to read. I hear that you're a good reader, Judith.'
Judith blushed, but picked up the story and read on in a slow but confident way.

Thomas saw Charlie glance out of the window. He followed his gaze and saw a delivery van arriving at the school. He waited a minute.

'Charlie.'

Charlie started in shock and dropped his eyes to the page before him.

'Charlie. Take over from Judith, please'.

Charlie immediately picked out a sentence at random and began to read. The other children sniggered in their relief that the Head's attention was now away from them.

'Judith has read that part already. Were you not paying attention?'

'I lost me place.'

Why did you lose your place?'

He shook his head.

'You weren't paying attention, that's why. I can see that the van in the playground delivering crisps and pop has more interest for you than the story of Our Lord.' The boy coloured.

'Read to us from the top of page seven.'

Charlie began to pick his way laboriously through the words, as if his feet were stuck in Thames mud.

'And…Joseph…Mary…and…the…baby…Jesus…took…to ok….'

He stopped and stared at the word, but couldn't work it out. He saw his friend, Peter, mouthing the words, flight…flight', at him.

'…took fright', Charlie said with relief.

'That's not the word! Look at it and think about what's happening in the story. The Holy Family are running away from King Herod who wants to kill them. So do you think the words are 'took fright!' Do you really think 'took fright' is good English! Think about it!'

Charlie felt his own anger rising. 'If he was coming after me to chop me 'ead off, I'd take fright alright!'

The children laughed, their sympathy now with Charlie.

'I would too an' all', said Peter. More laughter. As the children grew bolder; the tension evaporated from the room.

Thomas stared at the children until their laughter gradually faded.

'The word is 'flight'. 'Flight'. The Holy Family 'took flight' into Egypt, and away from the cruelties of King Herod.'

Charlie gazed through him to the wall beyond.

'Well! We are waiting for you to continue.'

The class stared at Charlie, who stared at the floor.

'We are *still* waiting for you to continue reading.'

'I ain't no good at reading. I don't want to read it!'

Thomas said quietly, 'Well, I'm sorry, but we all have to learn to do things we don't like. Life is not just about fun

and games. You are all here to learn, and that includes you, Charlie. So read on, please. Now!'
'Mr. Young don't make us do this!'
The class was quiet now, all eyes on Thomas.
'No! Well, I am sorry to hear this. Charlie, I'm not going to ask you again. Continue reading, please.'
'No. I ain't! When is Mr. Young coming back?'
Thomas ignored the question.
'Well if you don't, you will go and sit in my office and wait for me. And at the end of this class I will telephone your mother. And she will come here and collect you and take you back home. And that is where you will stay. Because I will not tolerate this disobedience from you, or anyone else. Now is that clear enough for you?'
They stared at each other, until Charlie, his face red with shame and anger, snatched up the book and mumbled his way to the end. The children sat in silence.

Chapter Seventeen

February: The Feast of Saint Sadoth

Jim Osborne waited in reception for Bryan to arrive. They had an appointment to meet Jo Fowler, the person appointed to be external investigator into the allegations. The company, an educational management consultancy, was located on the third floor of a modern block of offices; Jim had heard that Jo Fowler seemed determined to carve out for the organisation a reputation for investigating child abuse allegations.
He knew that Jo had attended conferences with Mary Edwards, the Lead Child Protection Officer, to present joint papers on key issues in sexual abuse investigation, and, as a result, authorities across London were beginning to call on her investigative services.

Jim thought glumly, 'I hate these cases.' He had only been with the Union a few years and was more at ease in negotiations with employers about conditions of service than in dealing with these matters. He had two children at primary school himself, and had to fight hard to suppress the thought that, 'where there is smoke…' In his teaching career, he had come across male colleagues who were suspect in their relationships with children, so he knew there were rotten apples and he had no objection to them getting kicked out of schools. ‘You just can’t tell,’ he thought. ‘Bryan Young looks a regular guy. But who knows?’

Bryan arrived; Jim was taken aback by his appearance. He had first met him a few weeks earlier when Bryan had been suspended, but in that time he seemed to have aged. His eyes were puffy, hair lank, and there was a puppetry to his movements, as if walking was an effort.

Jo Fowler called them into her modern office. She was in her mid thirties, smartly dressed in a dark trouser suit and white blouse. Her fair hair was cut short. Jim noted the view across the park, the deep pile carpet, the Modigliani print on the wall - and thought of his own dingy room, overlooking railway lines, at the local branch of his Union.

‘Looks like investigating child abuse is a profitable business’, Jim said.

She looked at him as if he was some troublesome fly buzzing at the window. ‘It’s not all we do’.

Another smartly dressed woman of a similar age sat in the corner of the room, and Jo introduced her as Melissa, her personal assistant, who would take notes of the discussion. Melissa glanced at the two men without expression.

Jo explained that she had been appointed by the school to continue the investigation started by Jayne Boyle, and that she would be liaising with the Lead Child Protection Officer for the district.

She looked at Bryan. 'I know this is likely to be a difficult meeting for you, but I will try to be as sensitive to your feelings as possible, although you know I will have to ask some quite probing questions.'

Bryan nodded.

'If you need a break at any time during our meeting, just ask.'

Bryan thanked her.

'The purpose of this meeting is to ask you some questions in relation to the investigation. This is part of a formal process and what you say today could be presented to a disciplinary hearing, so you need to be aware of this before making your replies. Is that all clear, Bryan? Are you happy with the process outlined so far?

Bryan nodded.

Jo continued, 'Before we move onto the specific allegations, I would like to gather some background information on your professional career in teaching so far.'

Bryan outlined his work to date, and told her about his role at The Holy Apostles.

'How would you describe yourself as a teacher, and how do you think other colleagues see you - and would describe you?'

‘I regard myself as a good teacher. I’m professional, and I am interested in - and always have been - in how children learn. I would say that I have a good rapport with my class, but I don’t allow the children to run riot. I keep order, but, at the same time, I try to be myself with the children and express my own personality. I would hope my colleagues see me as professional too – you probably know I am an Advanced Skills Teacher - so this has been recognized by the local education authority and the school.’

‘You say that you try and ‘be yourself’…and express your own personality with the children. Will you say a bit more about that, please, Bryan?’
‘I think… I believe, that children respond better to someone who can encourage them to laugh and relax, so that they enjoy coming to school. If they are at ease with their teacher, and respect him or her, they will not be afraid to attempt something new. I try and make learning as interesting as possible, but within professional boundaries.’
Bryan felt the emotion coming back into his life, like water flooding onto a parched land, as he described his work.

Jim Osborne listened. ‘He says all the right things,’ he thought. ‘But he has to.’ He had heard too much bull-shit in education to believe uncritically what people said.

Jo shifted the focus of the interview.'Who are your line managers, and how would you describe your relationship with them?'
'It would be the Head, Mr. Wood, and his deputy, Jayne Boyle.' Bryan hesitated, 'I haven't always seen eye-to-eye with them on discipline related matters. But I respect them for what they have achieved at the school, particularly the Head. You probably know it was in Special Measures before the Head took over, and things have obviously improved enormously since then.'

Jo paused. 'Bryan, let me outline then the nature, in detail, of the allegations against you first. Then I will ask you some specific questions to record your responses.'
Jim and Bryan became more alert. This was the first time either of them had been given a detailed overview of the accusations.
'Tracy Banks alleges that you kissed her on the neck, in the downstairs corridor of the school, on a Tuesday morning just before the start of a class led by Father Kelly. She also alleges that you told her you loved her and that you were in a state of sexual arousal. She alleges she saw this arousal through your clothing. How do you respond to this?'

Bryan felt as if he had been struck. 'It's completely untrue! I remember the class. Tracy was the last to arrive, and she was clearly upset about something. I was sympathetic to her, but told her we needed to talk later about whatever it was that was upsetting her. We then went into the classroom and Father Kelly started his class. The whole conversation couldn't have lasted more than a minute.'

'Did you touch her at any time during this conversation?

'I...I think...I remember touching her lightly on the shoulder to reassure her; a sort of 'cheer up' touch.'

'How would you describe your relationship with this child, Tracy Banks?'

'It's just a normal teacher to pupil relationship; nothing more - certainly nothing more!'

'But is it not true that you volunteered to give her extra tuition, after school hours?'

Bryan felt himself to be on marshy ground.

'No. I did not 'volunteer.' Mrs. Banks asked me if I would consider doing this, and I said we needed to talk about it.'

'And did you?'

'Yes. I went to see Mrs. Banks the following Saturday at her home.'

'It is a common school policy across the country - and the Head tells me it certainly applies at The Holy Apostles - that teaching staff need permission from a member of the senior management team for pupils to be given extra-mural help of this nature. Did you seek permission for this, or discuss it with the Head, or deputy Head?

Jim Osborne looked closely at him.

'No.'

'Can you tell us why not?'

'I realize now that I should have done. But I didn't think that there would be a problem with this. It was my time, and I was trying to help a pupil in my class – one who is struggling with her reading.'

'Is Tracy the weakest in your class with reading?' Jo asked quietly.

He hesitated again. It would be easy for her to check. 'No, but she is one of the weakest.'

'So why go out of your way to just assist Tracy Banks, and not the weakest in the class, or others as weak as she?'

He hesitated, 'I suppose, because Mrs. Banks asked me. She made a point of it.'

'I understand that you, Tracy, and Mrs. Banks danced together at the recent disco. Is that right?'

'Yes.'

'Did you know that photos Tracy took at the disco were placed on a social network site on the Internet?'

'The police told me something about that - I was very surprised, even shocked to hear it.'

'Tracy has put other photos and film clips of you on the same site. One film clip shows you dancing with a group of girls from the school in the playground. A boy is seen and heard in the film loudly insulting Father Kelly about his weight, although you don't appear to intervene or object to this. There is another brief film clip too, of you surrounded by a group of girls; Tracy Banks is among them and has her arm around your neck. She is saying that she loves you. You don't seem to be objecting to this, although the clip fades shortly after this. The Deputy Head has made a statement to me too, about writing done by Tracy, in which she says she loves you. She states that when she challenged you about this, and asked if you intended to follow this up with Tracy, you did not reply. She reported that you looked angry this had come to light.'

Bryan looked at her, stunned.

Jim Osborne had to make a conscious effort not to shake his head in disbelief at what he had heard. 'This guy has had it,' he thought, 'he's dead.'

Bryan recovered his wits. 'I can see where this is going. Tracy Banks is fixated on me; that's the only explanation I can give. I had no idea how far this had gone in her mind. But the allegation she has made about me – about kissing her, telling her I love her, and the rest – is just not true. And this incident with the writing; this has been misinterpreted. I was encouraging the children to differentiate and discriminate between extremes, love and hate, for example. I certainly did not exert any influence over what Tracy Banks wrote, and I certainly did not encourage it.'

‘I want to pursue this further, Bryan. Because the allegation has been made by Mrs. Banks that you told Tracy - in Mrs. Banks hearing, at the disco - that Tracy looked ‘sexy’ in her dress. Is that correct?’

‘I can’t rememb…no, no, of course I wouldn’t have said anything like that to a girl of nine - in her mother’s presence!’

‘Are you suggesting you might have done it if her mother had not been present?’

‘No! Of course I wouldn’t say such a thing to a child at all, ever! I remember now at the disco, her asking me if I thought her mum looked sexy and cool. I agreed that her mum did, and I said something about Tracy looking cool, but not about her being sexy.’

‘So you thought her mum, Mrs. Banks, looked sexy?’

‘I just agreed with Tracy’s verdict. I didn’t go out of my way to say this.’

‘Alright. So you went to see Mrs. Banks at her home. Was Tracy there when you arrived?’

‘No. She and her sister were both out.’

‘I understand you went upstairs and shortly afterwards you were found by Mrs. Banks in her daughters’ bedroom. Is that correct?’

Jim Osborne thought, ‘This can’t get any worse - can it?’

Bryan said, 'I did go into the bedroom, and I can see how stupid it was to do so without asking permission from Mrs. Banks. But I wanted to see how Tracy lived and to get some better understanding of what goes on in this girl's life. She can be rather a nuisance in the classroom - demanding attention - and I was driven by curiosity, and probably pity, for the girl.'

'Mrs. Banks ordered you out of the house at that point. Did you not try and give her an explanation along these lines?'

Bryan remembered that the police had asked him the same question; this would be a question in everyone's mind.

'No, she was too angry to listen to anything I had to say.'

'Mrs. Banks view is that you were just, as she puts it, 'snooping' in a young girl's bedroom.'

'I know how it looks, but it simply is not the case.' For one moment, he was tempted to tell them what had happened, but decided this would finish him off completely in their eyes, as well as probably destroy his relationship with Jennifer once it became public.

Jo poured some water for herself; she offered Bryan a glass, he shook his head. She looked carefully at him.

'Moving away from Tracy Banks, we come to a statement made by two other pupils, Latesha Harris and Millie Hughes, about an incident in a literacy hour class last term, when it is alleged that you pushed them into a corner of the room and spoke in a way that suggested you were sexually aroused. Latesha alleges that you said she was making it 'hard' for you, meaning, according to Latesha, that you were having an erection in her presence.'

Jo continued. 'They mentioned too, that you had brought a book into the class that showed sexually explicit drawings of men and women and that you 'talked to them about it.' How do you respond to this?'

For some unaccountable reason, Bryan thought of the scene in 'Alice in Wonderland' when Alice says, "You're nothing but a pack of cards". It seemed as if his life was like that pack that flew into the air about her. Except this wasn't a dream. It was happening to him, here, now.

'I said nothing of the sort. I remember telling these two girls off for bullying another child, Maureen O'Hara. But I did not "push them into a corner". I told them to come with me away from the other children, where I told them off. I may have said something to the effect that Latesha was making it hard for me, but this was about forcing my hand to talk to her mother, or the Head, about her. I reported the matter of the bullying to Latesha's mother later that day.'

'And as for the book', he continued, 'these are two separate incidents, not one. For a start, I did not "bring the book into class"; it has been in the class for months. The school approved the purchase of it, and it is used in schools all over the country. I found Latesha, Millie, Tracy Banks, and Annie Morris too, I think, sniggering over it at an earlier class. I remember deliberately *not* getting involved in a discussion about the pictures.'

'So you didn't touch either girl?'

Bryan suddenly remembered that he had taken Latesha by the arms to get her attention. 'I took hold of Latesha's arms and told her to look at me, as she was pretending not to care what I was saying by deliberately looking away.'

'Was that a wise thing to do?'

'Have you ever worked with a class of nine year old children?'

'We are not talking about me, but about what you did. I assume you know that schools don't allow aggressive physical contact of this sort.'

'Aggressive physical contact!' Anyone would think I was a yob on the rampage in that classroom!'

Jo paused, unruffled, and looked coolly at him. The temperature in the room had raised; she wanted a few moments of calm before she continued.

She continued. 'I do need to return to this issue of touching, and then focus on the issue of suggestive language with you. In the course of this enquiry, Jayne Boyle and I have been speaking to some of the children in your class, and to some of your colleagues. There are recurring statements about you touching children - and I am not saying in a sexual or aggressive way - but touching them on the shoulders, or holding hands. You have just mentioned that you touched Tracy on the shoulders in the corridor, and we have already discussed Latesha's and Millie's statements. You know the guidance for working practices on this matter: that this should be professional and strictly limited. What's your position on physical contact with the children?'

Bryan measured his words. 'I am aware of the guidelines, and I admit I over-reacted with Latesha. I normally only touch children when it's necessary to comfort them, reassure them, or keep in contact with them. For example, if I was listening to a child read, and was interrupted by another child, I might keep in contact with the reader, by placing my hand on his or her shoulder whilst I dealt with the interruption. But why are you are making an issue of this just with me? I can think of a dozen other teachers who regularly comfort children by touching them.'
'Alright Bryan. I have noted your point, but let's just stick with you. I want to move on to the issue of suggestive language. Your colleague, Helen Myers, has made a statement about a conversation you had with a group of girls in the playground. Helen has alleged that you encouraged

them to dance for you and said to them, "come on, let's see you all shake it".

Miss Myers interpreted this to mean that you wanted them to shake their bottoms.'

'Helen! Helen has said this about me! This is…incredible! I can't believe she would say this. The girls came up to us asking Helen initially if they could show us their dance steps. I said that they could, and 'shake it' meant their dancing steps, not their backsides! God in heaven! This is crazy! And Helen Myers…I've seen her with her arms around boys and telling kids she will kiss their bruises better! Are you talking to her about this, too?'

'As I said earlier, let's just stick with you, Bryan. I am interested in what you have done. This enquiry concerns allegations against you, not anyone else.'

'But that's all very well – but what about double-standards: one set of rules for men teachers, another for women!'

'Alright Bryan. We're nearly at the end.'

He felt his teeth grind at her patronizing tone.

'Finally, I want to ask you about your reaction when you were first presented with these allegations. The notes of the meeting record that the Head said, "*I've called a meeting because a serious allegation has been made against you – about inappropriate words and behaviour*". The notes record that you replied, "*Nothing happened; we didn't do*

anything together". Was this how you remember it, Mr. Osborne, you were there, I believe?'
Jim nodded.
'Can you explain your response, Bryan? What did you mean by "nothing happened"? And who were you referring to, as regards the "we". It wasn't clear who you meant?'
'I thought it was about…something unrelated to all this,' said Bryan.
'Would you care to say what?' Jo asked.
'No. It's not related.'
**

Bryan sat in Jim Osborne's office. 'What do you think, Jim?'
Osborne was unnerved by this case, only the second of this type he had dealt with.
The previous incident of a similar nature had resulted in the resignation of the male teacher before the hearing convened.
'I don't think this is looking good for you. If you want my honest opinion, I think you should consider resigning.'
He avoided eye contact with Bryan and continued quickly.
'If you resign now, you can avoid a disciplinary hearing. You can put this behind you. If there is nothing incriminating on your computer, the police are unlikely to take action, and the school will accept your resignation. You won't have a disciplinary hearing on your record.'

‘But I won’t be able to work as a teacher again. The school won’t give me a reference.’
‘Yes. That’s true. But you need to think about other types of work. Move on and away from working with kids.’
‘But I didn’t do anything wrong! I can see how things have come together like they have. But I swear to God I didn’t kiss Tracy, and I didn’t tell her I loved her. And Latesha and Millie are both lying through their teeth. I am not guilty of anything!’
‘Look Bryan. You are up against this investigator – she is obviously no fool – and she works closely with Mary Edwards, who has a national reputation for investigating child protection issues. I can see where they are taking this – the signs are they will be alleging that you were in the process of, well, grooming children… for your own… purposes.’ Jim shook his head, ‘It’s stacking up that way - certainly from the line of Jo Fowler’s questions. So you need to think carefully about going under your own steam now - before you are pushed.’

Chapter Eighteen

'Mum! She's pissed in the bed again.' Shelley looked at her sister with scorn. 'She stinks up the room!'
Della came into the room, 'For God sake, Tracy, not again.' She began to pull the sheets off the bed; an acid smell wafted from the rubber cover over the mattress.
'I can't help it!' Tracy wailed. Her pyjama bottoms, grey with wet, stuck to her legs.
'What do mean, you can't help it!' Della felt like slapping her. 'You used to get up before in the night, why do you have to piss the bed now? I have to wash this lot!'
She thrust the stinking sheet in Tracy's face, who sobbed louder.
'Go on, go and get washed! She'll be here soon.'
'I want to go back to school. I don't want lessons here. It's boring.'

Tracy had enjoyed the one-to-one attention of the home tutor at first, but this had soon palled under the close scrutiny of the teacher. Her friends from school had deserted her. No one had called to see her now, and when she went to Latesha's house, Latesha's mother had turned her away: 'Latesha is in enough trouble without you adding to it.'

She was still sobbing when she came back into the bedroom.
Shelley said, 'It's your own fault. Why did you say all that stuff? You're telling lies.'
'I ain't, I ain't.' Tracy shook her head. It had happened. The more she thought about it, the more real it became. The way he had looked at her; the nice way he spoke; the way he had gently touched her when she was upset that time in the corridor. He did love her, and he had kissed her. And she was glad he had.
**

The children gathered around Latesha and Millie in the playground.
'What have you been saying about Mr. Young?' said Peter.
'I can't say anything,' said Latesha, 'I've been told not to.'
She was enjoying her role as the keeper of secrets.
'I heard you'd said something bad about him,' said Peter, 'You grassed him up!'
Latesha glared at him. 'No I didn't, I just told them what happened that's all. Didn't I Millie?' Millie nodded.
'Yeah, well what *is* supposed to have happened?' The boy could see he was getting somewhere, and was determined to find out what and where. 'We've got stuck with 'pus and boils' now he's gone, thanks to you!' He meant Jayne Boyle, who had just been teaching them.

‘He did stuff to me, and said stuff. That’s all I can say.’
‘What stuff? You mean pervie stuff, or what?’
‘I ain’t saying. They asked me questions and wrote down what I said, and I bet he won’t be coming back, I can tell you that much.’
The power of this suddenly struck her with shivering warmth. She had been enjoying her role in putting a bossy teacher in his place; she imagined that in time he would come back to school and be a bit more careful how he spoke to her. But this, the idea that he was a pervert was something else, and much more interesting.
The children were quiet, struggling with the idea that Bryan had done something serious and wouldn’t be returning.
‘Yeah, well, I bet you’re telling lies,’ said her accuser. ‘He ain’t done nothing to me or anyone else I know.’
‘Shut your face! I ain’t telling lies, am I Millie?’
Millie shook her head.
**

Beryl, the school cleaner, moved through the staff room tidying up. She had heard that Bryan had been suspended. George, the caretaker had told her, and she slowed her actions to catch the talk. She was interested; she liked Bryan. He wasn’t as stuck-up as some of this lot. She strained to hear.

A group of teachers clustered together at a low table, their voices mingling.
'Helen had to make a statement. But she's not saying anything about it. She just says she can't talk about it, if you ask her.'
'I heard that children have made some allegations about him - about sexual remarks he's supposed to have made.'
'I can't believe it.'
'Well, who knows? Some of the girls in his class have been all over him in the playground. You just don't know to what extent he has encouraged this.'
'Yes, we saw him at the disco, with Tracy Banks and her mother.'
'Most of us were dancing with our kids. And Helen had her own group of lads hanging round and drooling over her half the night.'
'There's dancing and dancing. And there's talk about him even grooming children.'
'What talk? I haven't heard any such talk! Are we not letting our imaginations run away with ourselves?'
'Maybe, but Tracy Banks hasn't been at school for the last week. Joan in the office says she's having home teaching now.'
'What does Christine say about it? She seems to know him better than most.'

‘She’s not saying anything. I’m not sure she knows any more than the rest of us.’

‘It’s a pity. I feel sorry for him. He’s a good teacher. It’s all too easy for a teacher to be accused of stuff these days. There was that case in the Midlands. The teacher got sent to prison until it went to appeal.’

‘But that was with teenage girls. What do we really know about Bryan? He doesn’t talk about his life outside of school, and I think he’s just too familiar with the children. Yes, OK, you need to be friendly, but you need to keep your distance as well.’

‘Yes, especially if you’re a man in a school with girls on the brink of puberty.’

‘I heard there’s a woman investigator from an outside agency working on this. I saw her in school the other day, and wondered who it was. Joan said she was working with Jayne.’

‘It must be serious if the Head is spending school money on investigators.’

Beryl thought, ‘I wouldn’t have said he was the sort to mess around with children. But there’s no smoke without fire. If he has done it, he should have them cut off. There’s no excuse, none; in a Catholic school, too.’

She went off to report to George. George knew a regular at his local pub who worked for the district newspaper - he would be interested enough to buy him a drink for a story.
**

Jo Fowler conferred with Mary Edwards. Jo had heard Mary speak at a conference on child abuse, and had recognised the opportunity for the education consultancy company she partnered. Interviewing teachers suspected of child abuse was difficult and tricky for a school, as the accusation of bias could be levelled at them by either the accused teacher, or the parents of the children involved.
Jo had read widely on the subject, drawing heavily on Mary's past conference papers and published articles, before approaching her to offer independent investigation services to the schools in the district, and beyond.
Jo and Mary had now worked together over the last two years, with a string of successful results, where the teacher concerned had either resigned before a disciplinary hearing, or in its wake.

Mary summed up the situation so far. ' I've received a report from Social Services. After their initial visit they believe that the child, Adam, is in a 'low risk' category. But they'll be revisiting the home unannounced over the next few weeks and will review the case in three months time.

However, a disciplinary hearing at the school is another matter. From what you and the school have told me, there is certainly enough to proceed.'

'I would have thought so,' said Jo. 'As you know, the children concerned were interviewed by Jayne Boyle, and we have the transcripts of these meetings. I have also interviewed the Head and Jayne Boyle about Bryan Young's work at the school'

'Yes, they made for interesting reading. It seems as if Mr. Young was noted for his non-conformity. But that fits the pattern.'

Jo continued, 'The statements from Tracy and her mother to Jayne Boyle suggest that Mr. Young has been working his way into their affections over a period of time, which, of course, he denies. However, the evidence of the mother is particularly strong in this respect, particularly when she describes his visit, unsanctioned by the school to their home and him being found in the girls' bedroom. He alleges he was just getting an impression of the child's home environment.'

'Yes,' Mary said, 'This is an important issues. One would imagine that the mother would not have been so angry, if he had told her what he said to you at the interview. But he didn't. I have heard too, from her home tutor, Vanessa Horton, that Tracy is bed wetting, and that the child is consistent in her casual discussions with Vanessa about what happened.'

"I am not so sure about Latesha Harris and Millie Hughes though,' said Jo. 'Bryan Young is suggesting that the two girls are conflating two separate and unconnected incidents, and may be able to verify his side of the incident from other child witnesses in the room.'

'Well, children are often unsure of all the detail about times and days. I would be suspicious if they were. That's why we need to see this holistically,' said Mary. 'I believe there is a typical pattern of early stage grooming emerging here, although we need to be careful what we actually say at the hearing about this.'

Mary consulted her notes. 'I heard from the police. They found nothing on Bryan Young's computer and they feel they don't have enough evidence from just the written statements of the children to secure a conviction. He doesn't have a criminal record, apart from a driving offence when he was younger. However, the fact that nothing incriminating was found on his computer by the police suggests that he is likely to be at an early stage of development in all this. Men start abusive behaviour somewhere, and sometimes this is triggered by some significant event that releases feelings long suppressed. He became a father about eighteen months ago, and this can release sexual feelings about children. He cannot contemplate abusing his own child, so looks elsewhere. Previous cases of this type suggest that, when they start, they do it slowly and cautiously, building the trust of children in a steady way, and as you say, Jo, "working their way into their affections"; nicely put.'

Jo dropped her eyes in acknowledgement. Mary could be quite formidable, so she was warmed by the unexpected compliment.

Mary paused. 'So we need to look at other pointers emerging. His over-familiar talk with children, his implicit encouragement of discourteous conversations about other members of staff; his kicking against the rules; the encouraging of children to trust him - to dance for him - are key indicators. I think, in particular, the dancing is an important issue. The Findley case in the North of England showed that this is a way for abusers to encourage children to lose their inhibitions.'

Jo said, 'Yes, there was that other allegation in South London last year; just the same thing happened then.'

Mary nodded. 'Yes. There's also the issue with touching in this case. The touching of children, on its own, can be seen positively - and certainly will be presented as such by a defendant at a hearing. But, again, we need to put this into context with what else has happened. I think we have a strong case to present to a hearing, and I've just heard from the school that we now have a date'.

Chapter Nineteen

Jim Osborne put down the local newspaper. 'This doesn't help,' he said to Tom Watson, his colleague at the Union office.

> **Male Teacher Suspended**
>
> A male teacher at The Holy Apostles RC primary school, Green Lane, has been suspended following allegations of 'improper words and behaviour' toward pupils.
> Head teacher, Thomas Wood, confirmed that an investigation was in progress and an internal disciplinary hearing would be arranged.
> The police have been informed, but are not making any criminal charges at this stage of the enquiry.
> Derek Hartley, Chair of Governors, said 'Parents of children at the school have great confidence in the teaching staff here, and we are determined to pursue this matter in a vigorous and fair way'.

'Have you got a date yet?' asked Tom.

'Yes, at last: June 16th, at Ventura House; about time too, this has dragged on far too long.'

'What are the allegations specifically?'

'Well, basically, there are four. There's the allegation of inappropriate words and behaviour toward Latesha Harris and Millie Hughes. There's 'inappropriate words' again, in the playground, with this business about the girl's dancing, and 'shaking their bottoms' for him. Then there's 'behaving unprofessionally' by visiting the home of the Banks girl; and then there's the killer charge of 'inappropriate words and behaviour' toward Tracy Banks. All the other stuff they'll bring up will feed into these four allegations'.

'What line are you taking?'

'Well, it's stacking up against him. But we have written character witnesses from his previous school, including parents of children in his class there. I tried to get someone at The Holy Apostles to be a character references, but they're all backing off. He was pretty shaken by this; he thought at least Christine Evans would stand up and be counted for him.'

'They are all worried for their own jobs these days' said Tom. 'No one wants to get across the head teacher. You soon find out who your friends are in a case like this. He won't resign then?'

'No, I've suggested it twice, but he's not having it at all. And not after this,' he said, indicating the newspaper. 'He will fight it all the way.'

'Do you think he is in denial?'

Jim considered. 'I don't know, I really don't. At first I thought he was guilty as sin. But I just don't know anymore. The more I get to know him… he just doesn't seem the sort. But who knows? And with Mary Edwards on the case…it's the issue with him going round to the house and going into the bedroom - plus what the girl is saying happened in the corridor; those are the nails in his coffin. I'm going to have to play it by ear on the day; to be honest I'm not sure what I'm going to say!'

Tom said, 'Well, in my experience, I think he's best quitting now. You can never shake off allegations like these.'

Chapter Twenty

June 16th: The Feast of Saint Luthgard

Bryan dressed carefully. He had trimmed his hair and was wearing a grey suit and white shirt. He stood in front of the mirror carefully knotting his navy blue tie. He had spent most of the previous evening and early part of the night reading and re-reading the file of papers that had been sent to him. These were statements from the children interviewed by Jayne Boyle, Jo Fowler's interview transcript of her meeting with him, alongside transcripts of interviews with Della, Jayne Boyle, the Head, and Helen Myers.

He had read until the words, like the allegations, fused into one raging lynch mob against him. He had sunk eventually into a troubled sleep, but the dawn chorus had woken him around four. How could life bring you to such a dark place so quickly?

It had been over five months since he had been suspended. He'd had no contact with the school until the letter came with the date of the hearing. The police had returned his computer fairly quickly, and there were to be no charges brought by them. This had raised his hopes that the school would drop the matter. But the report in the newspaper had shattered these. Although he was not named, the parents and pupils at the school would know it was him, as he was the only male teacher there, apart from the Head.

He had spent his days with Adam and when it was fine would take him to the park, although he went in dread of being pointed out as a teacher accused of sexual offences. Once he had seen a pupil from his school in the park, but the child looked away and pretended not to see him.
It was the waiting, the waiting, the waiting - and the uncertainty of it all. The days went by, and he was conscious that in a corner of the district, the wheels of a system were slowly turning: people elsewhere had allocated a part of their time, a corner of their lives, to discussing his 'case' and preparing the documents for the hearing. However, these people could move onto other things, go home, watch their televisions, read their books, and forget about it. But for him, it filled his mind and pursued him and Jennifer relentlessly, all day and every night.

The day – this particular day, June 16th - would advance like any other. The individuals in the cast would all rise, eat their breakfasts, drink their coffees, and make their respective ways to Ventura House. They would all assemble at the agreed time, listen, or speak their allotted lines. The clock would go forward, the words spoken by the players falling into permitted time slots. Those playing the role of Governors would confer, give voice to their thoughts, and make their decisions. This same time tomorrow he would know his fate. All in the space of twenty-four hours, whatever the decision, his life would have changed, irrevocably.

Jim Osborne had telephoned him yesterday and asked him again if he wanted to resign before the hearing. But he clung to the thought that he had not done anything wrong with the children, ever. He had committed no wrong deed with any of them. He was guilty of wanting, once, to shag Della, or what he thought Della represented, but had quickly opted out when he had seen her close up.

He rationalised that Della would not want to admit to her part in this tragedy, and neither would he, and he had told no one of this. He believed that the Governors would recognize the truth when he spoke the truth - about not harming the children - and would allow common sense to prevail. He was a good teacher, an Advanced Skills Teacher, with character references. He had never been in trouble with the police. He had a female partner and a young son. He was not a paedophile, a sex abuser, a nonce, queer, poofter, pervert, shirt-lifter: the words from his childhood echoed around his head. He remembered the local scorn and abuse directed at the men who fell into these categories. He was not like that. He was a good man, and he would be believed. Good men are believed.

**

Lydia Cole, administrative clerk, grade 3, typed into her laptop computer that the Disciplinary Committee of the Governing Body of The Holy Apostles Catholic School commenced its business at 9.30am at Ventura House, June 16th. Lydia noted that the Committee was comprised of three governors: Mr. Paul Michael, Mr. Harry Bowen, and Mr. Derek Hartley (Chair). They were assisted by Ms. Katherine Andrews (Human Resources), and Mr. Peter Moreton, of Moreton and Clough, Solicitors for the local authority, "…both present to advise the panel".

Lydia recorded her own unobtrusive presence, and that the Management's case was to be presented by Mr. Thomas Wood (Head teacher), and Ms. Jo Fowler (Endeavours Educational Management Consultancy).

Lydia noted too, that Mr. Bryan Young, and his Union representative, Mr. James Osborne, were present, and that all parties agreed they were in receipt of copies of all the documentation relevant to the case, prepared for them by the management of the school.

Lydia noted too, but not for the record, that Mr. Bryan Young was a bit of alright, and that if he preferred to get it off with pre-pubescent girls, rather than with full-blooded and amenable women like herself, then God was having a bit of a laugh at his and her expense.

Lydia recorded that the hearing opened and Mr. Wood advised the members of the Committee that the children making the allegations would not be present as witnesses, as this was not permitted. He reminded them that the hearing was not a court of law, and that the Committee would have to decide if there were sufficient grounds to believe, from the evidence presented, that a breach of professional behaviour had taken place. The Committee were also advised that, although they had full transcripts of their statements, three adult witnesses would be called to support the management case: Mrs. Della Banks, mother of Tracy Banks; Helen Myers, teaching assistant at the school; and Mary Edwards, Lead Child Protection Officer for the local authority.

The Head explained that the Management would present its case first and then Bryan Young and his representative would have a chance to reply to all the accusations made. He pointed out that six character witness letters in support of Bryan had been received and these were among the papers presented to the panel.
Thomas paused. 'However, I feel it is my responsibility to say at this point that I, and the rest of the staff at the school,

have lost all confidence in Mr. Young. I feel he has acted in an improper manner toward the children in his care.'
Bryan felt the chill of his words, as all eyes in the room fixed on him. His left hand shook, and he took hold of it with the other to steady himself.

Thomas then asked Jayne Boyle, on his behalf and as lead internal investigator, to present the background to the case. Jayne retrieved her glasses from her chest and read from her notes. She outlined the circumstances leading to the investigation and her role in taking statements from the children involved, and also from Della Banks and Helen Myers. She told the Committee they would hear from Della and Helen later that morning.
Jo Fowler then took over. She summarised her interview with Bryan and referred the Committee to the interview transcript. She let them remind themselves of it for a few minutes before calling the first witness.
'I would like to ask Mrs. Banks to come forward and present her evidence.'

Della Banks came into the room. She was soberly dressed in a blue dress and fawn cardigan; her hair was swept back into a neat bun. She sat to one side of the Governor's table. Jo Fowler took her through the statement she had made with Jayne Boyle.

‘You said that Mr. Young had spoken to you about Tracy’s work, particularly her reading?’

‘Yes, that’s right.’ Della was making an effort to bring her accent in step with the middle class tones of her interrogator.

‘And that he offered extra tuition at home?’

‘Yes.’

‘What did you think about that?’

‘I was pleased he was showing an interest in Tracy.’

‘So what did you do?’

‘I invited him to my house.’

‘He came round to your home the following Saturday, at lunchtime, I believe. Can you tell us what happened then?’

‘We talked downstairs for a bit. But then he said he wanted to use the toilet and he went upstairs. But I heard the floor above creak, and that isn’t the toilet, so I went up and found him skulking around in the girls’ room. I realized then that he wasn’t up to any good and asked him to leave. When all this blew up at school, it all came out then - about Tracy being lured by him, and all the business with her phone, pictures and films on the Internet.’

Jo Fowler asked her, ‘How is Tracy now, Mrs. Banks?’

‘Very upset! She is stuck at home waiting for all this to finish. She has lost her friends, her confidence is gone. She’s been wetting the bed. Not surprising though, is it? She’s been betrayed by a teacher at her school!’

She looked across at Bryan for the first time in the hearing; she felt the frustrations of the last six months spewing up into her throat, 'You should be ashamed of yourself!'
The room went very quiet.

'I understand how upsetting this must be, Mrs. Banks,' said Derek Hartley, 'I'm sorry you are in this position; it is very difficult for you.'
Jo Fowler allowed the silence in the room to linger a while longer, eventually saying, 'I understand you overheard Mr. Young make a suggestive comment to your daughter, at the school disco. Is that right?'
'Yes. He said she was looking 'sexy.' Sexy! About a nine year old girl! I didn't think anything of it at the time. But I can see now what he was up to.'
All eyes in the room again turned briefly on Bryan.

Jo Fowler had finished, so Jim Osborne rose to his feet.
'Er, Mrs. Bank…'
'It's Banks, not Bank!'
'Sorry…yes, sorry, Mrs. Banks. Mr. Young states that it was you who asked him if he would tutor your daughter.'
'Well, it wasn't. It was him,' she said firmly. 'He came up to me after school and we got talking and he asked me then.'
'Had you met him before then?'

'Yes, I met him at the disco. He got talking to me during the break, and then he asked me and Tracy for a dance. He seemed alright, but I should have begun to hear alarm bells ringing then. I could see Tracy was swanning all over him, but I thought it was just a kid thing with her teacher. I know better now.'

'You said you ordered him out of the house when you found him in the bedroom. What explanation did he give you for being there?'

'I didn't need an explanation. I could see what his little game was. I could see it in his guilty face.' Again all eyes looked in his direction. 'I told him to clear off.'

'Mr. Young states that he went into your daughter's room to see what type of influences there were on her life, in order to know her better.'

'Oh yes! If you believe that you'll believe anything!'

Jim felt himself wilt under her scorn. He had found Bryan's explanation hard to believe himself, given the other things that had been said about him.

'Well…about him saying your daughter was sexy. Is it possible that your daughter said it about you and Mr. Young just agreed with this?'

'No, it isn't!'

'Well, Mr. Young's memory of this is that Tracy asked him if he agreed that *your* dress was 'sexy and cool,' and he agreed. And that he said something about Tracy's dress too, but meant that it was 'cool,' not 'sexy,' as you have suggested.'

Jim felt himself struggling over the complexity of all this. Who, or whatever, was 'sexy' and or 'cool,' the words had no place in the mouth of a teacher of young children. Jim had no spirit for this fight.

'I was there. I heard him. He's going to say that now isn't he? He'll say anything now he's been exposed for what he is.'

Helen Myers had also toned down her appearance. Gone was the spiky hair. In its place was a neat fringe, and she was wearing a matching top and skirt. The jewellery was also gone.

She avoided eye contact with Bryan.

Jo Fowler said, 'What can you tell us about Mr. Young's relationship with the children, for example at playtime.'

'He was friendly with the children, and the children liked him.'

'He was friendly with them?'

'Yes.'

'Have you ever seen him touching the children?'

'I suppose so, occasionally.'

'Can you give us an example?'

'Well…a girl came up once and swung on his arm…'

'Did he discourage this girl?'

'Not that I remember'

'Alright, anything else?'

'Someone might fall over and he would pick them up and comfort them, that sort of thing.'

'Comfort them?'

'Yes, maybe put his arm around them, give them a hug.'

'A hug. Alright, now, I would like you to tell us about the incident in the playground that you witnessed, and described in your statement to Miss Boyle. Tell us what happened, please.'

'Well, we were both on playground duty when a couple of girls came up and spoke to us, and wanted to show us some dance moves.'

'And did they?'

'Yes.'

'Did you agree to this?'

'Well, I looked toward Bryan, as he was senior to me.'

'So it was Mr. Young who agreed?'

'Yes.'

'What did he say to them?'

'He said, "Come on, let's see you all shake it.'

'Shake what exactly?'

Helen did not reply.

Jo Fowler hardened her tone, 'Miss Boyle, in her statement, said you believed he meant for them to shake their bottoms? Is that not correct? Is that not what you said?'

'Yes.'

'And you agree that is what you think he meant?'

'Yes.'

Jim Osborne felt on stronger ground with Helen. 'Are you on a temporary contract at this school Miss Myers?

'No.'

'Were you on a temporary contract at the time of this alleged incident?'

'Yes.'

'So you have been put onto a permanent contract between the incident and now?'

'Yes.'

Derek Hartley intervened. 'I'm not sure what your point is, Mr. Osborne.'

'I'm just establishing this teacher's employment status, for the record.'

'Well, I hope you are not implying anything else with this line of questioning.'

'I'm not implying anything. May I continue?'

Hartley nodded curtly, his mouth a thin line.

'Miss Myers, is it not correct that the two girls came up to *you* initially, spoke to *you*, and wanted to show *you* their dance steps, not Mr. Young?'

Helen hesitated, 'They spoke to us both and wanted to show us both. As I said earlier, Mr. Young was the senior staff member, so I let him make the decision.'
'Are you sure that's what happened?'
'Yes.'
'Now, this business about 'shaking it.' Could it have been meant in a general slang way, rather than in the specific and sexual way implied here at this hearing?'
Helen hesitated, 'I…I can only say what I heard.'
'Yes, but you said a few minutes ago that you interpreted this to mean that Mr. Young wanted them to shake their bottoms for him. Didn't you?
'Yes.'
'And do you still stick with this, or could there be a more innocent explanation?'
Helen was on the brink of tears. Finally she said in a low voice, 'I will stick with what I said.'

Mary Edwards came into the room. She was dressed in a dark jacket and skirt, white blouse and carried a leather attaché case. Her grey hair was cut short to frame her face in an oval. She smiled briefly at the Committee, and glanced quickly at Bryan. This was the first time she had seen him. She introduced herself and explained that her role as Lead Child Protection Officer was to review the evidence gathered

and present her professional assessment of it to the management of the school.
Jo Fowler asked her to summarise the result of her assessment. The two woman exchanged smiles.
Mary faced the three Governors and spoke directly to them.

'First though, as these are particularly sensitive issues, where reputations are at stake, I would like to outline my experience in this area of work. I qualified as a social worker with a CQSW qualification, which I later converted to a degree in applied social sciences, gaining an upper second class honours. I then continued to study for a Masters Degree in Child Protection, where I gained a distinction. After graduation, I worked for ten years in a number of social services residential homes for children, gaining promotion to team leader, then to head of section. I left social services to work in the field of child protection within education, and I studied for, and gained, a Master of Philosophy degree from the North East London University in child abuse investigation within an educational context. I am currently the Lead Child Protection Officer for the authority, but I have been consulted and engaged professionally by other London authorities; this has included leading staff training sessions, and I have given my professional advice in difficult cases on nine occasions over the last five years.'

She then summarized how she had got involved with this investigation.
'In particular, I have been asked to consider whether the allegations made against Mr. Young fit into a pattern of behaviour similar to behaviours used by people intent on, what is known as, 'grooming' children for sexual purposes.'
She continued to look at the governors as she spoke, carefully, quietly, drawing them into her thought process in a way that made them want to nod in agreement with her.
'By grooming, I mean the ways in which an adult might coax and encourage a child to engage in sexual behaviour with them. There are four elements to this process. I have summarized these in the appendix for you.'
The Committee all rustled through their papers. She waited until they had all found it.

Mary began to count on her fingers. 'First, there has to be a stimulus or motivation for the offender. Adult sexual interest in children can start in adolescence, but is often suppressed. However, the opportunity to work with children can re-awake these feelings. The adults in this situation are often in a position of power or control over children; they might be able, for example, to give specific commands that the children feel they need to obey.
However, the power can come in other ways too. The adult may exercise the power of personality - of charisma - over

children; may woo them, for example, by their open, approachable ways. They may even behave in non-adult ways to gain the trust of a child: by making childish jokes, doing child-like things, and by generally letting the child know that he - or she - is on their side; is on their wave length.'

She paused. 'We have to ask ourselves do we have this element, or the strong possibility of its prescence, in the case we are considering today? But I will return to this point later, if I may?'
She smiled at the Committee; they all nodded their agreement.

'Second,' Mary continued, 'the abuser needs to overcome any inhibitions or suppressed repugnance he or she may feel about thinking of children as sexual objects of desire. This can be done, for example, by suggesting that the child wanted the sexual contact, and had even initiated it. The abuser might typically say that the child pursued the adult for this purpose, did all the running, and made all the moves in the relationship. Again, we must ask ourselves had Tracy Banks reached a point of infatuation with Mr. Young, as a result of a situation engineered by him?'

Again she paused, looking away at some middle space between her and the Committee, as if in reflection. 'We cannot conclusively prove such a process happened, but we need to ask ourselves, in the context of other aspects of this case, if there is a probability or strong possibility here? Is there a pattern of behaviour? Are there planned connections between the incidents reported?'

'The third and fourth elements,' Mary continued, 'Are about overcoming barriers: respectively the barriers of environment; and the barriers of child resistance.
In relation to the environment - by which I mean the place where the encounters with a child take place - the abuser gradually becomes an accepted part of it. If it is an institution, the abusers are seen as a part of that establishment, but may present themselves as rebels; as 'breaker of the rules.' They may, for example in a school, act openly in a way that is contrary to, say, school regulations, codes of conduct, or the values of the institution. This puts them on a more equal footing with children - who may also be inclined, because of their youth, to kick against rules. This can lower the guard of children toward abusers.
So having gained the trust of the child, the final stage is toward a slow build up of physical contact with them. Typically at first, this is done by gentle touching, often accompanied with humour and banter. This touching might

be in the form of an arm around a shoulder, holding hands with a child, or stroking their hair. It is a reassuring and friendly touch that is presented initially by the abuser'.

She paused. 'However, this physical contact progresses, by degrees, toward more intimate and overtly sexual touching as the child's emotional barriers are lowered. At this point, in this situation, the child can become confused and distressed. Its behaviour can change. A quiet child can become loud or aggressive; a compliant child can become disobedient. There may be incidences of bed wetting, or wanting to avoid contact with the abuser.
In this case, Mr. Young was in a position of opportunity – working closely with children - and we have read statements to the effect that he has worked hard to make himself popular with them. Of course, most teachers would strive to make themselves agreeable to the children in their care. But we must ask ourselves here, did Mr. Young go beyond the boundaries of professional conduct normally expected of teachers? The statement from the Head suggests that he did, and, indeed, he had been admonished by him for this in the past.'

Again, she looked away, as if in reflection. 'Now, on its own, this 'pushing against the system' could be treated by a Head teacher as an internal disciplinary issue. But we have specific allegations from Tracy and Mrs. Banks to consider, as well as from Latesha Harris and Millie Hughes. We have also heard from Helen Myers, about how these boundaries were broken by him. Statements from other children, and from members of staff, show him as a particularly tactile teacher. Again, on its own, this is an issue for internal discussion, but in this case you must consider if it is part of a bigger, more connected picture.'

Mary picked up her notes, 'I draw your attention to the statements of Tracy Banks.'
The Committee rifled through their file to the papers.
'In both statements Tracy is consistent with her version of events and later, informally, gives the same account to her home tutor. She states that Mr. Young, in a quiet moment before class, kissed her on the neck, told her he loved her, and was in a state of sexual arousal. It is clear too, that Tracy did not object to this. Indeed, she welcomed it from him. We must ask ourselves how could this come about without the active encouragement of Mr. Young?'

She referred the Committee to more statements and waited until they had found them. 'Latesha and Millie too, claim that Mr. Young physically pushed them both into a corner and spoke to Latesha in a sexually suggestive way. Why would he do this? One explanation is that Mr. Young is

forced to change his tactics, and becomes more aggressive, when confronted by children who are actively hostile to him. Latesha claims too, that Mr. Young had previously brought a book into the classroom that graphically depicted male and female genitalia; a book that we learn was resisted as inappropriate by a number of staff, including the Head, his deputy, and the school priest, Father Kelly, but was championed by Mr. Young. Here is the book!'
She produced the book and put it on the table in front of the Governors. It opened at a page depicting, in full colour, the internal reproductive organs of a woman. Derek Hartley flushed and passed it on quickly to the Human Resources and Legal representatives from the local authority; the latter looked at it distastefully before passing it back.

'We have too, the statement from Mrs. Banks which alleges that Mr. Young made an approach to her with a view to gaining individual access to her daughter in her home. Here we have an important environmental factor to consider. Gaining access to a child's home, as a trusted adult, can be a significant move by abusers, as it gives their future presence legitimacy. But Mr. Young was found in Tracy's bedroom, and was ordered from the house. The trust cycle was broken between her and Mr. Young, and this made Mrs. Banks remember other connected events that she had previously

dismissed as harmless – the comment about Tracy being 'sexy,' for example.'
Mary paused and took a sip of water; she let what she had said so far sink in.

'Yet Tracy was still infatuated by Mr. Young to the point where she lingered in the corridor and welcomed the advances she said he made towards her. The trust was still there, and it can be argued that Mr. Young - frustrated by his encounter with Tracy's mother in her home - was advancing the level of his attentions toward Tracy more openly now on the school premises, where he still held power.'
She saw a flicker of doubt in some of their faces, but had anticipated this.

'Now you may think this is a risky strategy for a teacher: to openly behave in this way on school premises. But the risk is often part of the appeal for the offender, and I can illustrate many incidents of teachers behaving in similar ways on school premises, in classrooms. I have selected and listed thirty reported incidents in the London area alone over the last three years.' She produced a photocopied sheet for each of the Governors.
'As children become more aware of the dangers of sexual abuse, so the number of complaints against teachers has risen. Last year, in the London area alone, there were over

1600 allegations of abuse of power made against teachers by children in their care; a third of these concerned the sexual abuse of children. The incidents on the list I have given you are just a few examples of where sexual abuse took place within school premises, and often within classrooms, where other children were working'. She let them look at the list for a few minutes.

'Finally, I feel from my experience that Mr. Young was at an early abuser stage, but the incident at the house accelerated his actions toward Tracy Banks in school. Now, it is true that the police are not taking action in this case, but they are working to stricter and more onerous burdens of proof. Social services too, have decided not to intervene in the situation in Mr. Young's home, where he is a parent of a young child. We must hope, therefore, that all will be well here'. She looked briefly at Bryan; the Governors did the same.

She continued. 'However, in schools the Governing Body is concerned with ensuring that all staff work within professional boundaries - for their own protection - and certainly for the protection of children in their care. The issue for you is about professional behaviour or - and this is what you must decide in this case - the lack of it. You must ask yourself, is there a strong possibility that Mr. Young seriously abused the trust- the *privileged trust* - given to him as a teacher?'

She stopped, nodded a brief smile at the Governors, and then half turned to face Jim Osborne. She tried to keep her face from betraying the scorn she felt for him and his ilk. In her time she had faced more than a score of union representatives at disciplinary hearings like this, and most were out of their depth with anything except pay issues. As he shuffled his papers and avoided eye contact with her, she felt he would be no exception.

Jim felt awed; she intimidated him completely. He found a paper he had been fumbling for.
'You have given us some statistics, but the results of a survey done by my own Union show that, of the two thousand or so allegations against our Union members, over ninety per cent were found to be unfounded, being either false or malicious.'
'I know of this survey,' she replied calmly, 'But only a relatively small number of these concerned sexual abuse - and the majority of these were proven, and resulted in either dismissal from the profession, or the criminal conviction of the abuser.' She added after a pause, 'I'm a little surprised you didn't know this.'

Jim blushed, and was aware of smirks from the Committee members.

He replied with more heat than he intended, 'The important point though, is about false allegations. You are making serious allegations against Mr. Young on the basis of comments made by young children. Is it not beyond the realms of possibility that these children are either imagining what happened, or making false allegations?'

'No. It is not "beyond the realms of possibility", as you put it, that children can fantasize or tell lies about teachers. But sexual allegations made by children against their teachers are very uncommon - indeed, I would say extremely rare - and, unfortunately, we have tended in the past to ignore, or even punish children, who have made these allegations. I'm afraid what has happened in some Catholic institutions in the past bears witness to this.'

She could see from the corner of her eye the impact this had on the Committee members.

'And don't forget', she continued, 'It is not just about what *children* have said. We have heard what Mrs. Banks and Miss Myers have had to say, and also seen written statements from senior managers at the school, identifying connecting pieces of a particular jig-saw of motivation and behaviour.'

Jim seized on the jig-saw metaphor. 'Are you sure though, that the picture on this jig-saw adds up to one of sexual

abuse? Don't forget a man's career and reputation is on the line here!'
'This is for the Committee members to decide,' she answered, 'and the Committee must look at probabilities based on the evidence.'
Jim sat down, annoyed with himself. He had no other questions for her.

Bryan Young faced his accusers. The panel had been given a copy of a statement he had written in his own defence, summarizing his own version of events. This was his opportunity to present his case to the Committee.
But his heart rate increased and breathing became rapid; the words came out in a broken, panting rush.
'I have been accused of something terrible…awful… appalling. I am not guilty of any of this… I can't believe I am here, and that… this is happening to me!'
His panting overtook his ability to speak. He began to weep, and could not stop.
The Committee members looked on silently.
Lydia Cole glanced toward Derek Hartley, but he was staring at Bryan with a look of barely concealed contempt on his face. She took the initiative, 'Would you like a glass of water?' she asked.
'Yes...yes, please.'

He drank his water and composed himself. He had gone through in his mind a hundred times what he wanted to say, but here he was: shaking, croaking, snot rolling down his chin.

Eventually he said, 'Please, please read my statement. I completely deny the allegations made against me. If I had wanted to abuse children, why has this not come to light before?'

'I have been a teacher for over ten years, and I have always behaved in a professional way - a fair and decent way. I love my job. I would never harm a child, never. I just wouldn't.'

He could not continue.

Jim Osborne took over. 'You will see that character references for Mr. Young have been presented by teachers and parents from other schools and these show what a caring person Mr. Young is. As he said himself, why should this type of behaviour suddenly come to light now?'

He felt himself coming alive, sparked by anger. Bryan's collapse, and Mary Edwards's sneers, had galvanized him.

'Mrs. Edwards talks about 'patterns' and 'connections.' Well, maybe what we have here are a series of very separate and disconnected incidents that have been put into - or more likely forced into a so-called 'pattern.' We have got to protect children, yes, definitely, of course! But we have to protect the people accused of these things, and make sure we have enough evidence – *valid* evidence – *reliable* evidence - before we ruin their lives. We are faced here with powerful statements made by children. But what do we know about these children? To what extent have the enquiries of the investigators looked at their lives, and the background to their comments? What do we know about Tracy Banks? About Latesha Harris? Or even Mrs. Banks? What is going on in their lives that might have led them to say these things?'

Chapter Twenty-one

June 19th: The Feast of Blessed Humphrey Middlemore

The letter came.

'*I am writing to advise you of the outcome of the meeting held on Thursday June 16th at Ventura House...'* It ran to ten pages and outlined who were present at the hearing, the allegations made against him, and a summary of his own case.

Finally it arrived at its point, '*...the Committee has found all allegations proven against you...the Committee has also determined that the only appropriate sanction would be dismissal from your role as a teacher.'*

It concluded that, '*...you have a right of appeal against this decision...should you wish to appeal this must be done in writing within 28 days of the date of this letter, and it would be appreciated if you would please set out the grounds of such an appeal within your correspondence. The School are sorry to be losing a teacher with your abilities. However, your inappropriate and unprofessional actions have left us with no choice in this matter but to dismiss you forthwith.'*

A fog of despair enveloped him. He showed the letter to Jennifer. Jim Osborne had warned him that if this was the outcome, his wages would cease immediately and the financial implications of this chilled them both. Jennifer was still working, but her income alone was not enough to pay their mortgage.

'We'll be alright for up to a year, with my savings, and your money,' he said, but he did not feel any optimism: the future was unwelcoming. What type of job could he get now? His teaching career was finished. He had no other obvious skills that he could trade.

'We'll be alright,' she said, and took him in her arms. But she did not feel alright; she felt the same foreboding touching her. And she felt suppressed anger; anger with him for bringing them both to this dreadful place. But for now, she buried it.

The doorbell rang. Bryan opened it. Two men were there.

'Mr. Young?'

'Yes.'

One man immediately raised his arms. He was holding a camera and took Bryan's photograph.

The other said, 'I understand you have been dismissed from The Holy Apostles School because of 'improper words and behaviour.' Is that right?' Bryan saw he was holding a small Dictaphone.

'I don't have anything to say – who told you about this?'

The man continued as if Bryan hadn't spoken, 'Dismissal for improper words and behaviour usually means sexual stuff with the kids - or their parents. What have you been doing? It's better for you to say something. Just saying 'no comment' usually means "I'm as guilty as sin", I'm afraid.'
'I intend to appeal. I'm not guilty of anything. You can put that in your paper.'
'So, alright, but not guilty of what? It's best to be straight with us, and I'll make sure your side of it goes in the paper. If you don't, people draw their own sordid conclusions, don't they? That's what happens; that's life unfortunately.'
'I have been accused of something I didn't do. I'm not saying any more. As I said, I'm going to appeal.'
'Are you married?'
At that point, Bryan was joined by Jennifer at the door.
'What's going on, Bryan?'
'How do you feel about Bryan being dismissed from his job for sexual impropriety? Is it Mrs. Young?'
'Clear off! He hasn't done anything wrong!'
'Well, I believe you,' the reporter said, 'so why not give us your version of events, as…'
She slammed the door shut; a picture of herself, Bryan and Adam fell off the wall and smashed its glass on the hall sideboard.

'Oh Bryan, Bryan, *Bryan*!' she cried, 'Why has this happened to us? Why did you go round to that child's house? Why did you have to go into the bedroom? Are you telling me everything that's happened? She ran into the living room and sank to her knees, rocking on her haunches, her head in her hands.

He dropped down beside her and tried to take her in his arms, but she shook him off. 'Get away! What's happened to our life?' she cried, 'Why is this nightmare happening to us?'

Adam started to wail. Bryan picked him up and began to calm him.

'I need to tell her what happened,' he thought, 'I've got to, I can't carry on with this stuck in my head.'

He turned to talk to her, to tell her about why he went to Della's house, but he could not do it. It would mean admitting that he had lied to her, cheated on her. He dreaded her reaction. And he couldn't summon the courage to say the words aloud. They stuck in his throat as he watched her weep.

But he would tell Jim Osborne; he had to now.

**

Their daily local paper clunked through their door.

Teacher sacked for 'improper' behaviour with children

A teacher has been dismissed from The Holy Apostles Catholic primary school, Green Lane, for 'improper words and behaviour' with children at the school. The teacher, Bryan Young, of Cornwallis Road, refused to comment, beyond stating that he intended to appeal against the verdict of the disciplinary hearing. He is believed to live with his female partner and their son.

The head teacher, Mr. Thomas Wood, would not give details of the incidents, although parents at the school expressed the belief that a number of female pupils had made complaints about Mr. Young's behaviour.

Mr. Wood commented that the police had been informed about the allegations, but had decided to take no action. He said, however, that Mr. Young's actions amounted to 'professional misconduct' and that the school had no option but to dismiss him.

The stone came crashing through the window about three hours later. The glass shattered into a score of fragments that spread across their living room. Bryan raced to the window and saw two hooded teenage boys running away. One looked back and shouted, 'Fucking paedophile…you're dead!'
He went outside. '**Peedafile**' had been daubed across his door alongside a crude skull and crossbones. Neighbours were coming out of their houses, but went back inside

without a word when they saw Bryan. He went to the shed to find some paint.

**

Christine read the newspaper report and saw the photo of Bryan's haggard face peering around the side of his door. She had felt guilty for not contacting him and offering her support at the disciplinary hearing. When she first heard of the allegations at school she had shrunk away from them, and from him. She justified this by reminding herself that staff had been strongly discouraged from discussing the case with anyone outside the school, and told to refer any approaches from Bryan to the Head or Jayne Boyle.

She was still ambitious, still climbing the professional ladder, and to be associated with another teacher accused of sexual misconduct with pupils was not a good career move these days, particularly in a Catholic school.

When Jim Osborne had contacted her for a character reference to be presented at the hearing, she had promised to get back to him. But she hadn't, and had avoided his persistent telephone calls to the school until eventually they ceased.

Yet, but yet, she could not reconcile the allegations, emerging through the initial fog of silence, with her impressions of Bryan. The allegations against him had been made by Tracy Banks and Latesha Harris, with little Millie tagging on Latesha's coat-tails, backing her up. She had heard that Mrs. Banks had made some damning allegations about him, too. But she did not trust the girls, and had not formed a good impression of Della Banks during the times she had seen her at parents' evenings. She knew that since the news of Bryan's dismissal becoming public, Latesha had drawn around her a group of pupils, who other teachers reported to be increasingly wilful and provocative in class. Tracy Banks had returned to the school, but was withdrawn and now largely ignored by the other children. When told to pay attention in a recent class, she had blown up at Jayne Boyle, called her a 'fucking cow', and had ran from the room. Della Banks had been summoned, and Tracy taken out of school for the rest of that week. There was a tangible sense of restlessness among the children, and it was clear that Bryan was the centre of confused discussion in the playground.

Christine had always regarded Bryan as a good teacher. Caring and relaxed with the children, perhaps a bit too informal, but he had never encountered any discipline problems with them. He was easy to have around in the staff room, and she was drawn to his lack of deference to authority figures in the school. Sexual abuse was the last thing she would have associated him with. But she had attended a conference on preventing child sexual assault last year, and came away feeling alarmed and grubby by the stuff she had heard. A speaker from the USA had presented statistics showing that child abusers average seventy-three victims before they are caught, because of their expertise at hiding their behaviour, and because children were disbelieved or easily persuaded to silence by adults. Another speaker had presented a 'typical profile' of a sexual offender: male, ostensibly caring and compassionate, often in a position of responsibility in their work. The offender often sought out children from under-privileged homes and would try to develop special relationships with single parents to get close to their children. Once inside the child's home, they would use love as a tool to draw a troubled child to them.

When it all blew up at school, Christine wondered if she really knew Bryan: if his friendship to her was not another part of this pattern of behaviour. Was it merely a strategy: a 'keep people on his side' sort of thing? His informality with the children, his banter, fooling around, and jokes with them, became suddenly suspicious and sinister to her.

But the gut feeling that he was not like this surfaced continually, only to be pushed down by her. An expedient voice in her head kept telling her that he had been through a disciplinary hearing. He had been found guilty. And he had been dismissed. Forget him. He's history.

But she could not. Her instincts continually goaded her: 'he is not the sort to do this.' She also fancied him a little.

He was not above a bit of flirting with her, and she had caught him off-guard once, ogling her tits, the time she had been wearing a thin top for a PE classes. She knew, too, he had a partner and a child out of wedlock, although they both kept quiet about this at school. It just didn't add up: him a child abuser.

She had also overheard that prick, Derek Hartley, talking to Joan in the general office, when she had been doing some photocopying. Hartley had been saying that now Bryan had been dismissed, the school could use his salary to recruit a new teacher on the bottom of the scale, and the surplus would pay the cost of decorating some classrooms. He sounded quite cheerful at the prospect. Christine wondered if others on the management team shared his view - and if it had influenced their decision.

**

Thomas had spoken to a few worried parents on the telephone, but no one had removed their children from the school so far. He spoke in confident and measured terms to the parents. Bryan Young had been dismissed from his job because the school had serious concerns about him, and because the school was vigilant in these matters. The children's welfare was his number one priority. All was under control.

Although he was restrained in what he said, Thomas felt some quiet satisfaction at the outcome, and sensed that his own position in the school had been strengthened. But it had been a surprise seeing Bryan break down like that at the hearing. He hadn't expected that of him.

However, this unfortunate business now needed to be closed, and his immediate job was to recruit a new teacher to take over from Bryan; someone who would be a willing and unchallenging team player. He needed to talk to Jayne Boyle about this as soon as possible, so they could interview and recruit a teacher before September. It was good to have Jayne as his deputy; she had managed the incident extremely well. Yes, the publicity was obviously not good, but he felt that he was going to be able to use this unfortunate episode to his own advantage in the long term.

**

Father Patrick Kelly knelt in church. He tried to pray, but his confused thoughts kept returning to Bryan Young. The Governors had heard the evidence and had found him guilty of the sordid things he had been accused of with these innocent children. But he found himself continually reflecting on his own words. 'Innocent children'; but what did that really mean? His occasional glimpse into the worlds of these children had widened at the Christmas disco. They were on the brink of – or had crossed into – a world of the flesh, with all its power; a world that he had preferred to ignore. The case against Young was, of course, that he had abused his position, his power; had stepped over a moral line and was pulling children into his perverted sexual orbit.

He had heard what Mary Edwards had said at the early stage of the investigation, and Thomas had regularly discussed the case with him, showing him the statements taken by Jo Fowler. The Head was convinced about Young's guilt. And the priest had read, with burning shame, the newspaper report, and had to listen to and endure the worried comments made by parents with children at the school. The blessed name of the school - The Holy Apostles - was now linked with these allegations. He should have felt glad that justice had been served; but he could not, and he did not know why he could not. Something gnawed at him.

He struggled to understand his feelings. He had felt the warm sin of pleasure at the news that Young was gone - dismissed; sacked. The images on the film clip of the boy mocking him - with Young quite blatantly ignoring the comments - still rankled and wounded him. He remembered too, the incident in the classroom and the boy's insolent comments about Joseph, the husband of The Blessed Mary.

It was as if Young represented all the moral latitude in the world that the children craved, seized, and exploited. He felt too, that the allegations against Bryan Young were also, indirectly, including him in their mire. He was a priest, single, celibate; and for that reason, suspect. Suspect in the eyes of the parents; suspect in the cynical minds of all those who could not imagine anyone living a life without sex. The priest felt no sexual desire for children – or anyone. That side of his life, limited as it had been, belonged to the past. He lived now to serve God, and to pass that faith and love on to the children. But the dullness in the eyes of their parents, when he met them after Mass, told him that religion, for many, was a duty rather than a genuine belief. It was to the next generation he looked for a legacy to his work in the parish and the school. He prayed to his Confirmation Saint, Saint Jude, for support; to help him to inspire these children; to get them to take their faith seriously; to live in goodness. But the crush of the material world on them, and - he faced this now - his lack of personality to connect with them, depressed him. He suddenly knew why he was glad that Young had gone. The children listened to Bryan with an attention and interest that the priest craved. The guilt and loneliness of this revelation struck the man.

Patrick lifted his eyes to the cross, 'Dear Jesus, have we done the right thing?'

Chapter Twenty-two

Bryan met Jim Osborne and told him what had happened with Della Banks.

'You bloody fool. Why didn't you tell me about this from the start?'

'I know! I know! I didn't think it would end up like this. I thought I could just keep it quiet, and not have to tell anyone. I didn't think Della Banks would want to say anything about it, and I honestly didn't think I would be dismissed. I thought the whole thing would be seen for what it was. I just didn't reckon on the impact the child protection woman would have.'

Jim recognized the truth of this. Ever since the hearing, he had been fretting about his lack-lustre performance, about the sniggers from the panel, and the open disdain Mary Edwards had showed towards him. He felt, however, a sense that now there was something concrete they could use at the appeal, although he wasn't sure how yet.

Della Banks was not going to easily admit to this, but it was something: a start.

'Does your partner know about this yet?'

'No. Not yet.'

Well, you are going to have to tell her, surely?'

'Yes… I know.'

‘Right, well, that’s the price you are going to have to pay. Rather you than me. You know too, that once this comes out at the appeal, there could be another disciplinary charge against you, don’t you, assuming they believe you? I would imagine that chasing after a parent to give her one is likely to be listed fairly high up in the Head’s ‘Little Red Book of Don’ts’, wouldn’t you?’

Bryan smiled, despite the leaden feeling in his stomach.

‘Yes, but I don’t want a sexual abuser tag round my neck for the rest of my life. And don’t forget, I didn’t do anything about it. I got out before anything happened.’

‘Yeah, well, I’m not sure the disciplinary panel will think too much of it all, especially in a Catholic school. Isn’t ‘coveting your neighbour’s wife’ against one of the Ten Commandments?’

‘Yes, along with ‘bearing false witness,’ and there’s been too much of that, too!’

They both felt a surge of optimism.

‘Right,’ said Jim, ‘Our grounds for appeal are that we have new evidence to present in support of our case, but we won’t be specific at this stage. And we need to go through all the statements line by line to see what we have missed. You need to go over with me exactly what happened with Della Banks. And I need to do some serious research and digging around before I face Mary Edwards again.’

**

Maureen Briggs caught Christine's eye at the end of school. Maureen was upset and tearful and ran to her waiting mother. Mother and daughter embraced in a hug for a minute, Mrs. Briggs rocking her daughter to and fro to comfort her.

Christine approached, 'What's the matter, Maureen?'

Maureen shook her head. 'It doesn't matter.'

'Of course it matters. Is there anything I can do?' asked Christine, looking toward Mrs. Briggs.

'Maureen's been bullied again. It's that Latesha Harris and her gang. That girl's getting worse, ever since Mr. Young was sacked - more's the…' She stopped; she wasn't going to question the judgement of authority.

'Is this true, Maureen, about Latesha Harris?' said Christine.

Maureen nodded, her nose dripping.

'What is Latesha saying? You can tell me. Let's all go back inside.'

**

Tracy Banks asked Della, 'What does it mean by 'dismissed'? Isn't he coming back to school?'

'No, he ain't', sighed Della, 'I've told you! 'Dismissed' means he's got the sack, finished, end of story. Serve him right!'

'But I don't know what's wrong!' She started to cry.

‘The girls are saying I grassed on him and got him dismissed. They won’t talk to me now.’
‘Well… you did grass on him! But that’s alright. Good riddance. He shouldn’t have done and said what he did to a nine year old girl. He got his picture in the paper, too. I hope the local yobs make his life a misery!’
‘I didn’t mind what he said,’ said Tracy; it was all getting mixed and muddled in her head, ‘I don’t like it there now; I hate that Miss Boyle!’
‘Yeah, well…she’s a stuck up cow alright. But I told you, I don’t want to be dragged up to that school again, Tracy. You hear that?’
**

Bryan told Jennifer about Della and what had happened at the house. He had been dreading this moment, but saw that he had no choice. He could not look at her.
As she recovered from the initial shock, she quizzed him further. ‘Just tell me again why you didn’t sleep with her.’
‘When I got there I woke up. I saw her the grubby way she was, the sordid, scruffy house, the way she lived. I thought of you and Adam…’
‘Oh yes! You bloody hypocrite! You made love to me the night before you went round to her house. Are you saying that if she had lived in a nice, middle-class house, with flowers in vases, you would have slept with her? Would you

have thought about us then? No, I don't think so! You would have been round there every Saturday afternoon if she'd been more your type.'

She looked at him, as if for the first time. 'You rotten bastard! I have stuck with you through all this…this shit…my work has gone down the drain…you have a son under two, and you are already sleeping around…'

'I'm not,' he wilted under her attack, 'I didn't sleep with her, that's the point!'

'But you had it in your mind. She just gave you a few 'come on' signs - and you went. You went to sleep with her. You lied to me, and you've kept it from me until now - and you have only told me now because you don't have any choice. Where's your loyalty to me and your son? Where's your honesty?'

'I'm sorry, I'm sorry', he shook his head, 'It won't happen again. I promise to God!'

' That's it. This is the end for me. I've had enough. I'm taking Adam to mum's house. I can't live with you now. I thought you were a decent person, but you're not.'

'Don't go! I need you! I wish to God I'd never danced with her that night.'

'You should have thought more about needing me, when you were getting showered and jacking yourself up ready to shag her.'

'Don't go,' Bryan pleaded, 'I need your support now, more than ever before. I need you to believe in me!'
She shook her head, 'You're on your own.'
**

Jim Osborne found the house. He hesitated; this sort of Dick Tracy investigative thing was not his style. He plucked up courage and rang the door bell at the house next door to Della Banks. 'What if this gets back to Della,' he thought, and he wasn't even sure what he would say to the person who came to the door. A dog barked furiously, but there was no answer. Feeling relieved, Jim moved along a house and tried again. This time a woman came to the door and looked suspiciously at him, 'Yes?'
She looked ready to slam the door in his face.
'I'm … I'm a representative from a teacher's trade union and…'
'Do I look like a teacher?'
'No, no, I'm not recruiting! I'm really sorry to bother you, but I'm making enquiries about something that happened here, in this street, about six months ago, involving a male teacher; one of our members. This man here.' He showed her the newspaper photo, but concealed the headlines.
She looked at the picture. 'What's he done? Something mucky, I bet. And what's this all about?'

‘He’s been accused, unfairly, of something, and I’m representing him at a disciplinary hearing. I’m just checking out an incident he said happened, in this street, between him and one of your neighbours, Mrs. Banks, at number eight. There was some shouting at the time, and I wondered if you witnessed the incident?’

She looked again at the photo. ‘Yes. I witnessed it alright,’ she stared at him, weighing him up.

‘Look, I only want to find out the truth of what happened. I can assure you, I am not here to get Mrs. Banks into trouble.’

‘That’s a shame! You’d better come in.’

Chapter Twenty-three

October 10th: The Feast of Saint Cerbonius

Jim Osborne had requested that Father Kelly and Jayne Boyle be called formally as witnesses at the Appeal, and thus be excluded from the early part of the Hearing until they were called to give evidence. Thomas was worried by this, but agreed with the request. He was particularly bothered about why Patrick Kelly was being called. The priest had asked him twice recently, since the appeal date had been set, if he was sure that Young had been treated fairly. Thomas had assured the priest there had been a long discussion among the Governors about the evidence before they reached their decision.

Lydia Cole took up position at the side of the room with her laptop computer and recorded the names of those present at the Appeal, including the representatives from the local authority, Katherine Andrews from Human Resources, and Peter Moreton from the Legal department. Peter Foster had agreed to be the Chairman of the Hearing, supported by Ali Desai and Elli Curtis. Mary Edwards would join the meeting on day two to summarise again for management. All the members of the Appeals Committee had been presented with their bundles of witness statements and other documentation from the first hearing.

The appeal commenced with a summary, in Jayne Boyle's absence, by the external investigator, Jo Fowler, of the events leading to the first disciplinary hearing. As she spoke, she referred the Committee to the various documents in front of them, summarizing the contents and main points of each of the statements. When she finished, she nodded to Jim Osborne.

Jim Osborne rose. 'We intend to show at this appeal that a series of lies were told by children and adults - including Mr. Young - that led to his unfair dismissal.'

All eyes turned in surprise on Bryan.

'Yes. Lies have been told; lies that were either malicious in intent, or grounded in fantasy, or, in Mr. Young's case, used to try and escape from a situation of his own making.

So, yes, Bryan Young has told lies - and you will hear this from him and about the real reasons for him visiting the home of Tracy Banks. But I will argue that this behaviour, whilst unprofessional, does not warrant dismissal from post. On the substantive charges of sexually inappropriate words and behaviour toward children, he is not guilty. This is what we will show at this hearing.'

Lydia would have liked to have noted in her Minutes of Meeting that, "Mr. Jim Osborne, the Union representative, had found some balls at last"; she hoped he was right about Bryan.

Jim now reflected his new found confidence. 'We would like to ask Father Kelly some questions.'

Father Kelly came into the room.

'Father Kelly. Thank you for agreeing to help us today,' said Jim.

Father Kelly bowed his head in acknowledgement.

'I want to ask you about Bryan Young and about the day you spoke to his class. Tracy Banks has made allegations that on this day, just before your session, there was an incident with Bryan Young.'

'Yes?'

'You have known Bryan Young ever since he came to work in the school?'

'Yes.'

'How does he normally dress when he is in school?'

'Dress? Well, I'd say it was…casual,' said Father Kelly, puzzled at the question.

'Casual. Will you be more specific, please?'

'Well, he's not a collar and tie man. He normally wears jeans, and a casual shirt. He often wears a leather jacket in colder weather.'

'Does he wear blue jeans most days?'

'Yes, yes, I would say so.'
'The day you came to talk to his class - the day that Tracy Banks made the allegations - was he wearing jeans then? Can you remember?'
Father Kelly thought, 'No...no...he wasn't! I remember now, thinking that he looked smarter than usual.'
'Do you remember what he was wearing?'
'I can't be sure, but I remember now, he wasn't wearing jeans. I think he had on a white pair of trousers and a jacket over a blue or black shirt.'
'Thank you. This confirms that Mr. Young was indeed wearing white slacks, and not jeans.'
Peter Foster asked, 'Why is this matter an issue in this hearing, Mr. Osborne?'
Jim said, 'It is important, and I will come back to this point later. Please bear with me.'
'Father, on the day Tracy Banks made the allegation against Bryan Young, you were already in the classroom, prepared to start your class, and Mr. Young was in the corridor, waiting for the last of the stragglers to arrive after break, is that correct?'
'Yes.'
'Can you tell us about the last of the children to arrive? How many were there? Did they arrive in a group?'
'As I remember, there was a group of around three girls, then Tracy Banks came in, followed by Mr. Young.'

‘How soon after the group of three girls did Tracy Banks enter the room?’

‘It was soon after.’

‘What…seconds, minutes, how long exactly?’

‘Well… about half a minute or so; not long.’

‘How did she look as she entered the room?’

‘Look? I really didn’t notice.’

‘Would you have noticed if she had been displaying any extremes of emotion - for example, obvious pleasure, or distress, or obvious depression?’

‘Yes…yes, I suppose so.’

‘But she wasn’t showing any signs of extreme emotion?’

‘Not that I can remember.’

‘What about Bryan Young? What did he do when he came in the room?’

‘He asked the children to welcome me into the class, which they did, and then he went to sit at the side of the room.’

‘Was he behaving in any unexpected ways, or showing an unusual mood?’

‘No I don’t think so.’

Jim paused, ‘What are your own feelings about Bryan Young, Father Kelly?’

‘My feelings? I can’t see how these are relevant. It is the facts of the incidents that are important, surely?’

‘Father, I am just trying to establish how Mr. Young was regarded in the school. You are a significant member of the school, especially in matters of morality, and so your thoughts on the issue of his character are particularly important. I would be obliged if you would answer this question.'

Father Kelly spoke carefully. 'I understand that he has been well-regarded by most of his colleagues as a teacher until this incident. I have felt, however, that he was always a little lax with the children over, what I would call, Catholic values.'

'What do you mean exactly; can you give us an example?'

'Well… I have felt that he encouraged the children to be a little, let us say, 'loose,' regarding matters of discipline and respect for people in positions of authority or responsibility.'

Jim said, 'I'll come back to this issue of Mr. Young's attitude shortly. But there have been a number of incidents reported in the press in recent months about sexual abuse in Catholic schools, isn't that so?'

'Regretfully, yes. But most of these were a long time ago, and in residential schools.'

'Indeed. But, because of your position, I expect you have paid a particular interest to these cases and to the men implicated. Is that so?'

'Yes, that's probably true.'

' You made the point just now about Mr. Young's attitude toward people in authority. However, drawing upon the insights you gained about men implicated in sexual abuse incidents, it it your opinion that Mr. Young is the sort of man to behave in the way described by a few of the children in his class?'

The priest hesitated. 'Only God can read our souls, Mr. Osborne.'

'Yes. But you must have a view too, Father. You must have met a few sinners in your time!'

'That was an unnecessary and flippant remark, Mr. Osborne,' said Peter Foster, 'Father Kelly has given you his answer.'

'Well, I want to press the question,' Jim said firmly. 'Father. Putting aside how you feel about Bryan Young's laxity on matters of discipline, were you surprised that he - this particular man - was accused of these terrible things by children in his class?'

Father Kelly turned the question in his mind, "Was he surprised?" *And the devil taketh him up into an exceeding high mountain, and sheweth him all the kingdoms of the world, and the glory of them...*

'Yes. I was.'

Jim called for Jayne Boyle to give evidence.

'Miss Boyle, I want to ask you about your interview with the school teaching assistant, Helen Myers. Your statement reported that Miss Myers and Mr. Young were approached in the playground by a group of girls who wanted to demonstrate their dance steps. And we heard from Miss Myers to that effect.'

'Yes. That is correct.'

'Who were these girls?'

'I haven't their names.'

'Didn't you ask Helen Myers or Mr. Young to identify them for you, so you could talk to them about their recollection of events?'

'No. Miss Myers gave me a clear statement of what happened.'

'And she gave you her interpretation of what she believed Mr. Young meant when he said 'shake it.' Isn't that correct?'

'Yes.'

'I am intrigued as to why you didn't talk to the girls to find out what *they* believed Mr. Young meant by 'shake it.''

'I didn't want to expose the children anymore than was necessary to this type of questioning, as it can be very distressing for them. I had the statement from a responsible adult as to what happened - and her interpretation of the words used.'

'Yes, but surely you needed to check to see if this particular interpretation was shared by the girls on the receiving end?'

'I have told you why I did not. And the motivation of the speaker, Bryan Young, is the main issue here, surely? And we have a responsible adult's interpretation of this on record.'

'Yes, but without any additional evidence - particularly from the children on the receiving end of these comments - all we have is the word of one adult against another: one saying one thing; the other, something completely different.'

'The Committee will decide on whose version is the most convincing.'

'Indeed! Alright, I would like to change direction. What's your impression of Tracy Banks, Miss Boyle?'

'I think she is quite a vulnerable child. Before the incident she was rather demanding and attention seeking. Since returning to school, however, she seems to be isolated and withdrawn, and easily inclined to lose her temper. She has shouted and sworn at me, for example, when I asked her to pay attention. And her mother reported at the earlier hearing that she is now wetting her bed at night.'

'You say a vulnerable child; attention seeking, and so on. Do you think she is a child that is susceptible to adult suggestions and attentions?'

She looked across at Bryan, 'Yes. Most definitely!'

'Thank you, Miss Boyle. Now I would just like you to go over your statement about your meeting with Tracy in the presence of her mother. Please re-read these to the Committee.'

Jayne read through her statement. He stopped her midway.

'Miss Boyle, so Tracy reported that Mr. Young - in the corridor - just before class - had kissed her on her neck and told her he loved her?'

'Yes.'

'And your next comment was, "*Now Tracy, Tell me why you have drawn this*?", and you pointed to the drawing on the whiteboard. Is that correct?'

'Yes.'

Jim said, 'I find it strange that you did not ask Tracy to say more about the kissing; for example, why she thought he had kissed her at that time, in that place, and how she felt about it.'

'I was trying to establish what had happened at that point.'

'Well, the 'what' is always preceded by a 'why'- a reason for something happening - is it not the case? And the two are inseparable. Don't you agree?'

'As I said, at that point, I was just gathering the facts of what happened.'

'Alright, so you turned your attention to the picture on the whiteboard?'

'Yes.'

'So, Miss Boyle, let me be quite clear, Tracy replied to your question, about why she had drawn the phallus on the picture by saying "*… men's willies get hard when they like someone.*" Is that's correct?

'Yes.'

‘So then you said to Tracy, “*So are you saying that Mr. Young’s willy was hard when he was with you in the corridor?*” Is that what you asked her?

‘Yes.’

‘Don’t you think that your question, in the way you phrased it, could have put this idea into her mind?

Jayne was taken aback. ‘No, I don’t! Not at all!’

‘Why not? You have just told us that Tracy was “most definitely”, susceptible to suggestions made by adults. Surely your question was a leading one - a ‘suggestive’ one - was it not?’

Jayne fought back a feeling of being cornered. ‘No, it was not.’

‘Well,’ said Jim urbanely, ‘the Committee, in their good sense, will decide on this, too. In the meantime, I would like to move you on to the following sequence of question and answers from the transcript, about Bryan Young’s alleged state of sexual arousal. This was as follows; I quote:

‘Tracy, how do you know it was hard?’

‘I saw it.’

‘He showed it to you?’

‘Well I saw it. You can ask Latesha and Millie too, they know about it.’

‘Thank you, Tracy, I will. Are you saying it was out in the open, exposed?’

‘No, but I could see it was hard through his jeans.’

‘I want to be absolutely sure about this. This is a correct transcript of the interview, Miss Boyle?’

‘Yes. I have the tape if you want to hear it,’ she said impatiently.

‘Thank you, that won’t be necessary. Tracy says that she could ‘see it was hard through his jeans.’ But we heard earlier from Father Kelly that on this day Mr. Young was not wearing jeans. I believe you went to his classroom later in the day. Can you verify Father Kelly’s recollections about this?

‘I don’t remember what he was wearing.’

‘Oh! But Father Kelly - who probably saw less of Bryan Young than you did on that day - remembers clearly what he was wearing – because Mr. Young *wasn’t* wearing his customary jeans…but you say you don’t remember?’

‘That is correct.’

‘Would you agree, however, that it throws doubt on what Tracy Banks has said?’

‘That is not for me to decide. But children, whilst remembering the bigger picture, cannot always remember the fine detail.’

‘Children can fantasize too, can’t they? Haven’t you come across this in your career?’

‘We have moved on in society from dismissing serious allegations made by children as mere fantasy; weren’t you aware of that, Mr. Osborne?’ she asked, in an attempt to

copy Mary Edward's mocking strategy from the first hearing.
Jim was having none of it this time. 'I would like you to answer my question, Miss Boyle. I repeat, haven't you in your career come across instances of children fantasizing events?'
'You are suggesting Tracy Banks is fantasizing. Where is your evidence?'
'You haven't answered my question. I hope the Committee will make a note of this.'

Jim paused and checked his notes. 'Now I want to ask you too about your interview with Latesha Harris. The transcript records the following:
Latesha says, "*He grabbed me, pushed me in a corner, and said I was to look at him because I was making it hard for him*".
And you said, "*What do you think he meant by 'making it hard for him*?"
And Latesha says then, " *I suppose it was about his willy getting hard. That's what he wanted me to look at, weren't it, Millie, you thought that too, didn't you*?"
Now at this point, you go off at a tangent and say, "*How do you know about these things, Latesha, ... about men's bodies*?"

And Latesha replies, "*Mr. Young brought a book into the class for the bookshelf, with pictures of men and women with nothing on, and he has talked to me, Millie, and Tracy about it.*"

'Now it seems to me, Miss Boyle,' said Jim, 'that your logic is very flawed. You add two and two and get seven. Because Latesha talks about this book, you seem to automatically accept that the expression 'making it hard for him' means something sexual. Is there not another explanation for this term, such as "Latesha, you're a pain in the neck and you're making life very hard for me"; is that not another reasonable explanation?'

'It was Latesha who reached this conclusion…' Jayne started to say.

'…and it was *you* who accepted this as the "gospel truth according to Miss Latesha Harris", aged nine, who, as we will soon hear, is a school bully! However, I want to ask you about some procedural issues.'

Jim flicked through his notes, 'You were appointed by the Head to be the school investigating officer into what happened, is that right?'

'Yes.'

'So how many times did you contact Mr. Young during his suspension to see if he was alright or to tell him what was going on?'

'I did not contact Mr. Young during his suspension.'

'Oh! And why not?'
'I would have been happy to talk to him at any time, but he did not contact the school, so I assumed he was alright.'
'But you did not bother to find out?'
'As I say, I would have responded to any question or enquiry from Mr. Young, but he did not contact me.'
'But he was advised at his suspension not to make contact with his former colleagues - so was it not your responsibility to keep in contact with him?'
'I have given you my answer.'
She glanced at Thomas for support; he looked coldly back at her.
Jim continued. 'What did you think of Bryan Young when he worked here? Did you like him?'
Jayne was taken aback. 'I try to treat all my colleagues fairly… I don't have favourites at the school…' she floundered.
Jim shook his head dismissively. 'Alright, Miss Boyle, that's all.'

Jim said he would like to call a witness, Christine Evans, who would present some new evidence. Peter Foster conferred with Thomas, Katherine Andrews and Peter Moreton. He said at last, 'As this is new evidence, the Committee should have had the chance to read it before the hearing.'

Jim replied, 'I apologise for this, but the information has only recently come to our notice. We have prepared a written statement by Christine Evans and copies can be given now to the Committee.' Lydia distributed these.
Christine Evans came into the room; she caught a glimpse of the Head's tight face.
Jim said, 'Miss Evans, can you tell the Committee why you are here today?'
'I have been speaking to a child and her mother at the school, and the child's allegation has made me seriously doubt the allegations made against Bryan Young by Latesha Harris and Millie Hughes.' Christine paused.
The Committee were listening closely to her.
'Please carry on,' said Jim.
'The girl I spoke to is Maureen O'Hara, and she was in class the day the incident occurred that led to the allegations by Latesha and Millie. She told me that Latesha was passing round a bullying note about her in class and that Bryan Young saw this and intervened. She said that Bryan ordered the two girls to follow him into the corner of the room, but that he didn't touch them at this point. I understand that Latesha, supported by Millie, is saying she was manhandled by Bryan into a corner. But Maureen told me this didn't happen.'

Christine continued, 'Maureen saw Mr. Young speaking to Latesha and Millie in the corner, and she said that he looked cross with them, although she couldn't hear what was being said. At this point, and only then, Maureen saw Bryan take hold of Latesha's arms, and Maureen says she thought this was because Latesha was ignoring what he was saying. The conversation only lasted a minute or so and the two girls returned to the table. Maureen told me that Latesha was angry and just stared at her in a hostile way for the rest of the class - which upset her and led to Bryan trying to comfort her during break.'

Jim said, 'Thank you for that. And I believe there is something else?'

Christine said, 'Yes. Maureen has been bullied by Latesha and her friends for some time, and she said the situation has worsened since Mr. Young was suspended.

Latesha, according to Maureen, has been emboldened by her part in Bryan Young's suspension, and has been openly boasting to the children in her class that the other teachers would all be too scared to pick on her now!'

Christine continued, 'Maureen is a shy and withdrawn girl, and I only found this out because I saw her crying when she came out of school. Her mother was with her, so we both coaxed her to speak. Maureen has been upset by Bryan Young's absence, as she says he was one of the few teachers in the school that showed any real interest in her and who she felt she could talk to.'

Thomas felt the shock of these words; Ali Desai and Elli Curtis looked curiously at him.

Christine continued, 'I also wanted to come here today to speak up for Bryan Young. I feel rather ashamed of myself for not coming forward to say this at the first hearing, but I guess, like others in the school, I didn't know what to believe. And, if I was honest, I didn't want to get involved. This was made easier for me too, by the Head and his deputy telling staff they should not have any contact with Bryan and that we should report to them if he tried to make contact. Like a lot of people, when this stuff blows up, you think, "a man choosing to teach young children" - is there a more sinister motive?'

She looked across at Bryan. 'But the more I have thought about it,' she continued, 'the more I feel that Bryan Young is not the sort of person to do the things he has been accused of by Tracy Banks. He is a committed teacher, who gets good results from the children, and I just feel it's not in his nature to behave like this. His personality is probably more childlike than is good for him, particularly in a school where that sort of…spontaneity is not exactly the norm'; she felt and glimpsed Thomas's eyes fix on her, '…and it has made him more vulnerable than most to accusations like this.'

'I think the accusations are, well, just fantasy on the part of Tracy. She's a girl who seeks attention from adults and from her peers, and I think she is having trouble separating out what is real - and what she *wants* to be real. And as for Latesha Harris, I believe from what Maureen O'Hara has told me, that she is just telling lies and that the girl needs help.'

Helen Myers was called. The Committee was reminded by Jo Fowler of the main points from Helen's statement, particularly her interpretation of what Bryan had said to the dancers.

'Miss Myers, at the last hearing Miss Fowler asked you the following question; I quote from the transcript: "*Miss Boyle in her statement said that you believed he meant for them to shake their bottoms? Is that not correct*?"

Jim continued, 'And you agreed with this. The transcript records you saying 'yes' in reply.'

Helen nodded, 'That's right.'

'Can you remember exactly what Miss Boyle said to you at the time; can you remember how she phrased her question to you?'

'Well, we were talking about what Bryan Young had said to start the dancing, and Miss Boyle said something like,"Did he mean for them to shake their bottoms?", or words very similar.'

‘So it was Miss Boyle who suggested ‘shake it’ might refer to shaking their bottoms. Is that correct?’

Helen agreed.

Jim said, ‘So can you remember what your exact reply to Miss Boyle was?’

Helen nodded. ‘I said, “Yes, I suppose he did”.’

Jim said, ‘ “I *suppose* he did”. That doesn’t sound a particularly ringing endorsement to me. Why did you use the word ‘suppose’?’

Helen looked uncomfortable. ‘Well, I guess it was because - although there could have been another explanation - the likelihood was, that he meant for them to shake their bottoms.’

‘So there was a possibility, in your mind, when you spoke to Miss Boyle, that there could have been another explanation?’

‘I supp.... Yes!’

‘Then why didn’t you qualify your answer to her?’

‘I....because I was presented with an explanation for what he had said that seemed plausible in the circumstances.’

‘...And because it seemed to be the answer Miss Boyle wanted?’ said Jim, with some passion.

‘No! No, that’s not the case at all.’

Peter Foster quickly intervened, ‘Mr. Osborne! You need to be careful about making these allegations.’

Bryan felt himself choking with emotion and searched for words to express out loud his anger, but Jim jumped in first.

'Bryan Young has been living with false allegations made about him for almost ten months. This Committee should think about that!'
The room went silent.

Jim turned back to Helen Myers, 'Did you know the names of the girls who came up to you and Mr. Young in the playground?
'Yes.'
'When you were interviewed by Miss Boyle, were you asked to give her the names of the girls who danced for you and Mr. Young?'
'No.'
'Didn't you think that unusual?'
'I don't know… I haven't been involved in this type of enquiry before; I don't know what the procedures are. I would have given her the names if I'd had been asked, but I wasn't.' She was close to tears.
'I want to ask you what you feel about touching children yourself. A lot has been made about Bryan Young making physical contact with the children. Please tell us where you stand on this issue - how do you feel about making physical contact with children?'
Peter Foster intervened. 'Miss Myers is not the subject of this investigation, Mr. Osborne.'

'I'm trying to establish the extent of physical contact with children made by other teachers in the school.'
Without consulting the legal representative, Peter Foster said, 'The question is not relevant to this enquiry. Please move on, Mr. Osborne. Let us stick to Mr. Young and his actions, please!'

Jim decided to ask Bryan to speak as the last witness in the morning session.
'Bryan,' said Jim, 'I said at the start of the hearing that you had told lies - about your reasons for going to the home of Tracy Banks. Please tell the Committee about this.'
Bryan spoke quietly. 'At the school disco I met Della Banks for the first time… we got on well…I was physically attracted to her.'
Lydia typed this in, and thought, 'This is getting interesting!'
The Committee looked closely at Bryan, their faces a mixture of shock and disapproval.

'I saw her again, the following week, waiting at the school to collect Tracy, and we got into conversation. She said that Tracy needed help with her reading and asked me if I would tutor her. She asked me to come to her house to discuss it. However, I was getting signs from her that she was interested in me.'
'By interested, you mean sexual attraction?' said Jim.

'Yes.' Bryan glimpsed Jayne Boyle's glacial face from the corner of his eye.
'So what happened when you went to the house? Jim said.
'I went to the house anticipating that Mrs. Banks and I would…would sleep with each other. These were the messages or signals in my head that I had picked up from our previous meetings. But when I got there, I found I couldn't go through with it. Mrs. Banks was…well, seemed to be willing, but I…I didn't want to. I just went off the idea. I knew it wouldn't work, and that it was wrong in every sense to be there. I was downstairs with her, but I needed time to think. I made an excuse to use the toilet and went upstairs. I did go into the child's bedroom, but it was because, until then, I hadn't any idea about the sort of background Tracy came from. Mrs. Banks came into the bedroom - and she invited me into hers. I went, and she made sexual advances to me there. But by this time I just wanted to get out and I told her I had made a mistake. She was furious with me - and I got out fast!'

Jim pushed him further, 'Why have you not said anything about this before?'
'I didn't want to destroy my relationship with my partner. And I thought - obviously naively now - that common sense would prevail at the first hearing, and the Committee would

not find against me, and I wouldn't have to mention all this. But that didn't happen.'
Jim consulted his notes, 'When you were suspended, you said to Mr. Wood that, "Nothing happened. We didn't do anything together". Is this incident at the house what you were referring to when you made this remark?'
'Yes, it was.'
Jim said, 'Have you told your partner at home about this?'
'Yes.'
'And what has been her reaction?'
Bryan reddened. 'She has left me, taken our son, and gone to live in her parent's home.'

Thomas rose from his seat. 'I find it hard to believe what I am hearing. These are serious - *very* serious - accusations to make about Mrs. Banks – a parent at the school. She is expected here as a witness this afternoon and, no doubt, Mr. Osborne will want to put these matters to her. Are you sure you want this Committee to record what you have just said, and for Mrs. Banks to be subjected to this type of questioning?'
Bryan confirmed that he did. 'It's the truth, I'm ashamed to say.'
Thomas stared at him in disgust.
Peter Foster said, 'It looks like we have no choice'.

Jim continued, 'Mr. Young has said that this is the truth. This hearing is about getting at the truth, is it not?'

No one spoke.

'Alright,' continued Jim, 'Now the day that Father Kelly came to your class. Can you confirm that you were wearing white slacks, and not jeans?'

'Yes.'

'You normally wear jeans to school?'

'Yes.'

'So why did you wear slacks on this particular day?'

'It was because Father Kelly was coming to my class. The last time he came, with the Head, relations between us were somewhat 'strained.' So I wanted to start off on a better foot with Father, and I had dressed in a way I thought he would approve of.'

Jim nodded. ' Alright; now Tracy Banks says that you kissed her, told her that you loved her, and she alleges that you were in a state of sexual arousal. What do you say?'

'I completely deny this. It is simply not true. Tracy has made this up. I realize now she was in a world of her own, and I was at the centre of her fantasy. I bitterly regret going to her house. But I did not, would not, behave such a way towards this child – or any child.'

'So what about the allegations made by Latesha and Millie?'

'Latesha is telling lies, and Millie is going along with her. Latesha is talking about two separate incidents, which she has cleverly brought together in her statement to Miss Boyle. In the first incident, Latesha, with Millie in tow, was bullying another child, and I told them both off. I made the mistake of taking hold of Latesha's arms during the process, but this was to gain eye contact and get her to listen to what I was saying, as she was being deliberately provocative. But I realize this was a big mistake now. I said she was making it hard for me – but not in the sexual way she alleges. Making things hard meant how she was forcing me to discuss her bad behaviour with her mother.'

'You know what the school policy is about this? About referring such incidents to the Head?'

'Yes. Again, I realize I made a mistake. I know I should have taken this to Mr. Wood, but I prefer to try and sort these things out myself, if I can.'

'Alright, carry on.'

'In the second incident, Latesha and the other girls were already reading the book, and had chosen it themselves from the book trolley. Latesha tried to engage *me* in a silly discussion about the contents, and about men's bodies. I ignored this, and steered her away from the subject. I certainly did not 'talk to her about it,' as she says I did.'

'Now what about touching the children – you have already described what happened with Latesha – tell us about your attitude toward physical contact with the children.'

Bryan turned toward the Committee and spoke directly to them. 'I do touch the children – I physically comfort those who fall over, and keep physical contact with children if I am interrupted whilst listening to them read. In my previous school some of the younger children liked to sit on my kneewhen reading to me. I felt OK about that. All the teachers I know in primary schools have some physical contact with children; it's part of the territory; it's human; it's…it's *normal*, for heaven's sake! *Normal!* Helen Myers touches the children. But she wasn't allowed to answer Jim Osborne's question. Why not? This is not fair. All of a sudden, this issue of touching has become twisted against *me*. It has become 'part of a pattern'; an 'indicator'; a sign that I am a sexual predator. I am not. I am a good teacher…I…'

He felt himself becoming overwhelmed again, and deliberately stopped, remembering his breakdown at the first hearing. He shook his head and said quietly, 'All I can do is appeal to your common sense.'

He sat down.

Chapter Twenty-four

Della Banks was dressed neatly in a dress and cardigan; her hair was tied into a bun at the back of her head.
Jim asked Della asked her if she had received a transcript of her evidence at the first hearing, and if she agreed with it.
She nodded in confirmation.
Jim felt his nervousness returning as she glared at him.
'Mrs. Banks,' he said, 'I would like to ask you about your personal situation. It *is* relevant to this hearing,' he added hurriedly, as he saw Peter Foster looking sharply across as if about to intervene.
'Is Mr. Banks living with you at your home address?' Jim asked, holding his breath.
She bridled. 'What's this got to do with anything?'
'I would be grateful if you would answer my question. I just want to get a sense of your personal situation…'
Peter Foster intervened, 'I don't see why Mrs. Banks' personal situation is of interest to us, Mr. Osborne.'
'I think this will become clear if you will allow me the chance…'
Peter Foster held up his hand and shook his head, despite the legal representative's attempt to catch his attention.
Jim ignored this and persisted, 'I just want to establish if Mr. Banks is living in the family home.'
'He's working in Germany, if you must know!'

‘How often does he come home?’ Jim felt the hostile eyes of the Committee and Della Banks on him.

‘This is quite *enough,* Mr. Osborne,’ said Peter Foster, ‘Your question has been answered.’

Jim felt things slipping away from him, but he was not going to be deterred this time. He ignored the Governor. ‘You said at the first hearing that it was Mr. Young who approached you to offer extra tuition after school hours to Tracy?’

‘That’s right. It was!’

He paused, it was now or never. ‘Mr. Young, in his evidence this morning, said he felt that you were physically attracted to him - and that he was to you.’

He carried on quickly, ‘He said you invited him to your house, and his instincts were that you and he could…’

‘Could what? Could what? What are you insinuating?’

‘…could get together…sexually. He said that *you* made a sexual advance toward *him* at your house, which he rejected, and he left at this point.’

Della turned to Bryan, ‘You snivelling liar! How dare you say these things … to save your filthy skin! How low can you get? You’re not satisfied with wanting to abuse little girls - you’ve got to pull other people into your dirt!’

She turned to the Committee, ‘Are you going to let him say these disgusting things about me?’

Peter Foster turned to Katherine Andrews and the legal representative for help, but before anyone could intervene, Jim said, 'But it's not just Mr. Young who is saying this.' Della was listening like a fox.
'One of your neighbours was witness to Bryan Young leaving the house, and she heard what you were saying.' Jim produced a piece of paper. 'I interviewed the neighbour and she made a statement. Here is a copy.'
'Who…what *bitch* is saying this?'
'The neighbour said that you were shouting at Mr. Young, to the effect that he wasn't a proper man…'
'That's right! He's one that abuses young girls…'
'But the neighbour remembers you shouting about something else; more about his…manhood. You are quoted as saying that he, Mr. Young, "can't get it up." Why would you shout that at him?'
'I didn't! I was shouting, all right, but I was telling him and everybody else he was a pervert, which is exactly what he is!'
'So you weren't physically attracted to Bryan Young then - or angry with him because he rejected your sexual advances?'
'No!'
'But isn't it true that, shortly before he came to the house, you told someone you were physically attracted to him.' Jim paused. 'I have a written statement from a parent who met

you at the school disco, and this woman said you were making suggestive comments about him. She said you had even given him a nick-name: 'Mr. Yum-Yum'!'
'Then she's a liar!'

Christine's discussion with Maureen and her mother had led her to talk to Maureen's new friend, Tanya, and eventually on to Cheryl, Tanya's mum, about the conversation at the disco. Christine had passed this on, and Cheryl had reluctantly agreed to give Jim a statement.

'So,' Jim said, 'everyone's lying: Bryan Young, your neighbour, and now the other parent you met at the disco? Isn't it true, Mrs. Banks, that it was *you* who invited Mr. Young to your house, and because he rejected sexual advances *you* made toward him, you have made these malicious allegations?'
'I can't believe this! These are dirty lies! And you lot just sit there and let him say this… this… *filth* about me!'
The Committee sat in shock at her onslaught, appalled at what they were hearing.
Della continued in full flight now, and sensing she was gaining some advantage, she turned to face Bryan '…He calls a nine year old girl 'sexy'; he kisses her, tells her he loves her - with his cock sticking halfway up his trousers at

her! No wonder he has resorted to these dirty lies to save his skin!'

Jim did not allow himself to be overwhelmed. 'Well, let's talk about him saying that Tracy was 'sexy.' You say he said it at the disco, is that right?'

'Yes!'

'Well, Mr. Wood and Miss Boyle - and Father Kelly - were all standing just across the hall from you. So why didn't you go and report it to one or all of them if he said it and if you took so much exception to it?'

'I told you all last time, I didn't think about it until later, when it all came out about him.'

Jim pursued her, 'And you categorically deny you were attracted to Mr. Young?'

'Yes, I do!'

'But there are people, including members of staff in this room, who saw you dancing with him at the disco. Smiling and laughing with him; eating with him at the break. And there is a picture taken by your daughter - that was circulating around the Internet at one time - of you and him standing close together and looking very friendly indeed!'

'He was my daughter's teacher. I wanted to be friendly with him for her sake. But that's different to saying I was after him for sex. That's his dirty, twisted mind talking, trying to wriggle out of this.'

She turned to Thomas, her instincts leading her. 'I'm going to write to the newspapers about this! You allow this stuff to go on in your rotten school; just what sort of head teacher are you! I'm not taking any more of this!'
She left the room sobbing loudly into her handkerchief.

The room was left in shocked silence. Peter Foster conferred briefly with the others and adjourned the session for a break. When the Committee reconvened, Jim asked the Head to summarise his written statement, taken by Jo Fowler, about the steps he had taken following the allegation. Thomas went through the main points, outlining who he spoke to, when, and why.
Jim referred to his notes, 'We heard from your deputy, Miss Boyle, that you appointed her as the liaison person between the school and Mr. Young. We heard too, that she did not contact him once, not once, during his suspension period. Did you know that?'
Thomas shook his head. 'I know it now.'
'And what about you? Did you ever contact Bryan Young at any time during his suspension to give him an opportunity to state his side of the case to you?'
'No. Mr. Young had an opportunity to give his version of events to the external investigator, who then reported to me on what he said.'

Jim paused. 'What was your estimation of Mr. Young's teaching abilities before he was suspended?'
Thomas said, 'There are two levels to this...'
Jim audibly sighed.
Thomas ignored this. 'Firstly, there is his ability to prepare a lesson, keep order in the class, and deliver that lesson in an efficient and effective way. In this respect, I have no complaints about him, although there have been occasions when I have questioned the relevance and suitability of his teaching methods.'
Thomas paused. 'However, in regards to the wider issues of discipline – in the sense of upholding Catholic values, or inculcating children with a respect for order and the experience of age and maturity, I would say his attitude left a lot to be desired. Indeed, we have disagreed on these matters on a number of occasions.'
'Disagreed...could you give us some examples of areas of disagreement between you and Mr. Young.'
'Well... teachers should be role models for children. This involves gaining their trust and respect. You do this - in my book - by behaving like an adult. You don't do it by adopting the mannerisms of children, or by sharing inappropriate comments and humour with them, or by pretending, or hoping, that they are more intellectually mature than they really are. I think Bryan Young fell into these traps.'

Jim nodded, 'I certainly agree with your use of the word 'trap'! These 'traps,' as you put it, have branded him now as a sex abuser. Sometimes traps catch the wrong animals, wouldn't you agree, Mr. Wood?'
'We are dealing here with serious allegations made by children. The Child Protection Officer has presented her summary of the way patterns of abusive behaviours can be linked, and her experience cannot be ignored.'
Jim paused. 'I hope this Committee has noted how Mr. Wood avoided answering my last question. But coming back to Bryan Young, the man, did you like him?'
Thomas shook his head, exasperated. 'Liking or not liking doesn't come into it. The issue for me is to what extent a teacher is successful in his or her role, which is to help children grow into responsible, unselfish, moral adults. I think Mr. Young was only partially successful in this task before these hearings, and now….this whole sorry episode in the school's history has greatly saddened me. It has smeared the reputation of the school, its teachers, and the Catholic faith. And what has been presented here today - the sordid, grubby allegations made by him against Mrs. Banks, also fills me with …disappointment. Am I expected to 'like' someone who has brought us to this place?'
Jim raised an eyebrow, 'So your answer is 'no'?'
'I have given you my answer.'

'Well, you are 'saddened' by this whole affair, that's a shame! How do you think Bryan Young feels at being on the end of these false allegations since January; his name in the papers, no income, windows smashed?'
'Bryan Young had been accused and, I must remind you, found guilty at the first hearing of the worst possible crime, in my book - that is using his power to abuse a child. That is why we have taken these allegations seriously. What would you have us do, Mr. Osborne? Cover these things up, ignore the children, or worse, punish them for speaking out, as has happened in the past? No! We are here to safeguard children, and that is what we have been doing!'
'Oh! A fine, noble thing to do indeed, Mr. Wood,' said Jim, and immediately regretted it.
'No! Not noble. Honourable; the right thing, I think.'

Jim let the temperature cool a few degrees before he spoke again. 'Head teachers are important aren't they – to steer a school?'
'I think so.'
'Teachers climbing up the career ladder need to keep on the right side of head teachers, don't they?' His voice started to rise as he remembered battles with head teachers in the past; battles that had led him into trade union activity.
'What are you implying, Mr. Osborne?'

‘That many teachers toe the line with what a head teacher wants, and that a teacher who stands up for him or herself against a head teacher can be branded a trouble-maker, a loser, a pain in the backside, or whatever dismissive term serves the head teacher’s purpose. Disagreeing with a Head certainly won’t do a teacher’s career any good, and a head teacher can make his or her life, let’s say, ‘a bit difficult’; or do I have that wrong?’

‘You seem to be implying that I have a vendetta against Mr. Young. I resent this, and advise you now that this is an issue I intend to take up with your Union at regional level. Allowing you some latitude with your questions to witnesses - to ensure an impartial hearing - is one thing, but turning these proceedings into a soapbox for your personal or political views is quite another!’

Chapter Twenty-five

When Jim arrived at the start of the second day, Mary was deep in conversation with Jo Fowler.
He was nervous. The vehemence of denial by Della Banks had undermined him, and he was not sure if Bryan's confession about what had happened at the house had made any difference; it could have sunk him even deeper into the mire.
Jo Fowler called the meeting to order and summarized briefly, without going into too much detail, the events of the previous day. She called Mary Edwards to summarise her role in the investigation.
Mary repeated, in the same self-assured way, what she had said at the first hearing. She emphasized that her summary of events for management was based on an established model, well-known to professionals who worked on sex abuse investigation. '…This model helps to explain the process of child sexual abuse and guides us in looking for the patterns I have just outlined.'

Jim rose to question Mary.
'This model. You described how it outlines four preconditions for abuse, and the first of these, as you said, is motivation, when a child sex abuser gets arousal from

thinking about children. Does the model explain how and why someone gets to be like this in the first place?'

'No, it is a useful framework for identifying abuser behaviour patterns, as I said.'

'Well, surely we need to look at Mr. Young's past more closely, don't we - to see if there have been any clues from his history about his tendency toward this type of behaviour? Don't we need to ask ourselves if there are any reasonable grounds to believe that he *was* motivated in the first place to behave in the way you think he has?'

Mary Edwards stood quiet, assured, waiting calmly without commenting. She did not respond to his rhetorical questions, which rattled him, but he continued.

'We will hear later from two of his teaching colleagues, including the head-teacher from his last school, who will tell us there was no hint of abusive behaviour toward children when he was there. There are no police cautions or criminal convictions against him. And, significantly, social services have deemed him a safe and fit parent. Until recently, he was in a long-term relationship with a woman, and they have parented a child. Mr. Young was not abused by his parents, or anybody else, when he was younger. He simply doesn't fit the pattern. And even Father Kelly - who has had reservations about Bryan Young's attitude to authority - has said he was surprised by these allegations. Where is his ‘motivation’ to start abusing children?’ This time he stopped and looked directly at her, waiting for her answer.

‘I said at the first hearing that abusers come from all walks of life - there is no one defining or typical set of personal characteristics, although research gives us indicators and clues as to the social backgrounds of offenders. But as to motivation, I will not speculate about Mr. Young; I am not a psychologist, but I do know - from long experience of working with offenders - that they often conceal, deep within themselves, negative, destructive, and sometimes even evil thoughts. For the most part, they suppress these, or just turn them into internal fantasies that harm no one. But sometimes, these can come to the surface - triggered by an incident - or by an opportunity that is presented, or sought after.’
She paused. ‘I have looked at the statements of the children involved - and looked at other related incidents involving Mr. Young - and linked these with what is known about abusive behaviour, and you have the summary of my experience - over twenty years now in this field of work.’

‘But we must ‘speculate’ about Mr. Young,’ said Jim. ‘You say there is no defining or typical set of personal characteristics for abusers. Well, let’s look at that. I have seen research, conducted only a few years ago, that showed over sixty-five percent of the men involved in sexual abuse had offended in this way by the age of 21, which suggests they were actively engaged in this behaviour from a fairly early age.'

Yes, I know the research,' Mary said. 'But that still leaves a significant percentage of men *not* in this category and who remained below the radar until they were caught…and, staying with this same research…' Jim caught his breath, wondering what he had missed, '…forty-two per cent of the men,' she continued, 'had a reputationfor being, what is commonly known as, 'touchy, feely' with others.'

She continued, 'A number of children have reported that Mr. Young is tactile in this way, and he has also displayed on a number of occasions, boundary-violating behaviour: the dancing in the playground, inappropriate conversations with children, allowing himself to be photographed in a compromising way, the turning a blind eye to discipline infractions that should have been challenged by a responsible adult - and certainly by a professional teacher.'

Jim pursued this, 'Shouldn't a teacher in a primary school be prepared to physically comfort and reassure children? Mr. Young said earlier that this is part of the territory and, from my own teaching experience in the classroom, the younger children welcome it; it is an extension of the physical love and responsible care expressed by their parents, surely?'

'Of course, but there must be clear boundaries to this.'

'Yes,' said Jim, 'and there seems to me to be double standards in operation here. What is perfectly acceptable for women is regarded as suspicious if done by a man.'
'Men *do* have to be more careful than women, I accept that,' said Mary, 'and the boundaries *are* different. But is that such a bad thing? The reasons are bound up in the inescapable facts - that the majority of child sex abusers are men.'
'Women have been convicted in the courts of sex abuse of children too, so there shouldn't be these double standards - this is the point I am making.'
'And I repeat that the *majority* of child sex abusers are men - so men need to be more careful in their words and behaviour with children in their care.'

'Alright,' said Jim; he felt like Sisyphus. 'Let us have a close look again at the two main allegations made by the children against Bryan Young. First, let's look at the incident in Tracy Bank's house. You will, no doubt, have been made aware of what was presented yesterday in this hearing. Bryan Young has admitted that he was physically attracted to Mrs. Banks - *not* her daughter - and he states that he was encouraged in this by Mrs. Banks. He maintains it was she who invited him to her house, and that he went initially in the expectation of a sexual encounter with her. But he states that he had second thoughts when he was there and left the house before anything happened between himself and Mrs. Banks'. He produced the statement from Della's neighbour

'Some evidence,' he continued, 'was presented from a neighbour who testified that Mrs. Banks was shouting at Mr. Young - not in anger about her daughter and him - but in regards to his shortcomings - in her eyes - as a male lover to herself!'

'Yes,' replied Mary, 'I was made aware of this. And I understand that Mrs. Banks vehemently denied this version of events. But does it really explain his visit to the child's bedroom? The reasons for his visit to the house may be disputed, but what he alleges happened there - his admitted lack of sexual interest in the adult - is also consistent with a psychological explanation for abuse of children, in that some men feel anxious in their sexual encounters with adults, so turn their attentions to children.'

'But,' Jim persisted, 'as I stated earlier, Bryan Young has been in a relationship with the same woman for over ten years - and they have a child.'

'I understand that his partner has now left him.'

Jim changed the focus. 'I put it to you that one of the most significant aspects of this case is the accusation made by Tracy Banks against Bryan Young. We heard yesterday about inconsistencies in the detail of what she said happened. She said Mr. Young was wearing jeans, when in fact he was wearing white slacks. We also need to consider her background: what's happening, or not happening, in this poor girl's life, that she gets to a state where she makes up a story about an adult she obviously likes, if not 'loves.' In this case, the story concerns her young, male, attractive teacher, who I would guess, is probably about her father's age; a father who is not around, or so it seems. I was unable to pursue this issue yesterday - I was stopped from doing so - but it is something I intend to address later in this hearing.' He looked pointedly at Peter Foster.

'Tracy Banks is a vulnerable child,' said Mary. 'We know this from the school. But, as I have said before, vulnerable children are, unfortunately, the ones most often targeted by abusers. I would remind you all, that this only came to light when Tracy was seen to be drawing on the whiteboard and was questioned by Miss Boyle. You can say this was a fantasy. But it can be argued that what she drew, and what she said, was something very intimate and private to be shared only with her friends, but which she was forced to reveal when confronted by a teacher.

And I have said before,' she continued, 'we have dismissed, far too often in the past, allegations of abuse made by children as fantasies or lies. Children, in my experience do not lie about sexual assault - they don't have the language or experience, or motive to do this. Children may also get the details confused because of the traumatic nature of what happened to them. But Tracy has remained generally consistent in her version of what happened and we need to look at the incident in the context of other incidents and behaviours involving Mr. Young.'

'I believe that Tracy *wants* to believe it happened,' said Jim, 'and I feel sorry for the girl; she is not malicious, but she is immature… confused… and she has problems that have come to the surface in this destructive way. You just said she "is a vulnerable child". Did you not think of suggesting to the school they refer Tracy to social services for a family assessment?'
For the first time Mary looked uncomfortable. 'No, I did not feel this was necessary.'
Jim sensed her discomfort, and seized on it. 'Oh! Why was that?'
'I was satisfied that Tracy had been interviewed by Miss Boyle in a proper and professional way.'
'You were! Well, I'm afraid I disagree, and I hope the school will consider a referral in the light of our discussion.'
He looked at the Committee and let that sink in.
'Now I would like to look more closely at the allegations made by the two other girls, Latesha and Millie, I believe here we move into different country - malicious allegation territory!'

The Committee listened intently to him. 'We heard yesterday from a teacher at this school, who presented evidence from a child in the same class who witnessed the incident in question. This child strongly disputes the version given by Latesha and Millie and, in fact, throws considerable doubt on Latesha's statements. It appears too, that Latesha is revelling in her powers as the new Witch-finder General for the school!'

'With respect, Mr. Osborne,' Mary said, with an expression that denied her words, 'I understand that the child did *not* hear what was said by Mr. Young to Latesha and Millie in the corner of the room. And, as I understand it, she has her own agenda, and perhaps a score to settle with these two girls. We need to treat what she said with caution…'

'And surely that same…same *caution* should be applied to what Latesha and Millie said,' exclaimed Jim in exasperation. 'This is what I simply can't understand! Latesha has admitted her dislike of Mr. Young. Maybe it's payback time, as far as she is concerned!'

'Payback time! I assume that means, in English, 'taking revenge,' she said dismissively. 'Unfortunately, that's an adult notion, Mr. Osborne. You should not transfer such devious adult motives so easily to children's behaviour.'

Jim felt drained; he had no more questions for her. In the silence that followed, the sounds from an adjoining room filtered through to them – people talking, laughing, waiting for their working day to end.

Jim called two witnesses to speak for Bryan. The head teacher from his last school spoke about how he had trusted Bryan on residential school trips with the children, and how highly Bryan was regarded by parents.
Bryan's old teaching mentor, Anita Rowe, who had supported him during his early years in teaching, described his personality as, "a bit off the wall", but confirmed the children liked him, and enjoyed having him as their teacher. 'I just do not believe these allegations,' she said simply at the end of her statement.

The Committee was flagging as Jim stood to summarise. The room was stuffy. Peter Foster fidgeted; he needed to pee. Jim emphasized the lack of any evidence of motivation on Bryan's part to abuse children, the lack of police action, and the lack of action against him by social services.
He presented examples of teachers who had been accused of similar behaviour by children, only to be exonerated after experiencing a long and highly stressful period of enquiry. He reminded them of the witnesses who had come forward since the first hearing to support Bryan, and of the professional character references that had been given for him. He emphasised that the Child Protection Officer, had

never met Bryan Young, or any of the children involved in the allegations, and was simply relying on the statements taken by others.

'Finally, I want to bring to your attention irregularities in these procedures that we will take to an industrial tribunal if the decision goes against us today.'
The atmosphere suddenly changed; the Committee became alert. Thomas who had been sitting with his eyes closed, tapping his fingers impatiently on the desk, looked sharply up at him.

'Firstly, we heard from Miss Boyle, the investigating officer at the school, that she did not contact Mr. Young at all, not at all, during his period of suspension. However, the guidelines governing procedures in these matters clearly state that the named contact, Miss Boyle in this case, should, I quote, " *regularly update the employee about the case*", and " *keep the employee up to date with work activities*". The school has been completely negligent in this respect.'

Jim looked at Thomas. 'Secondly, as far as the Head is concerned, the guidelines are quite clear on his management responsibilities, which are, I quote, to "*...have a duty of care toward their workers and should act to manage and* *minimize the stress inherent in the allegations and disciplinary process*".

Jim paused and looked at the Governors. He continued, "*throughout the process the individual should be aware of the concerns and why his/her suitability to work with children is being questioned and given the opportunity to state his/her case with anybody involved in the decision making process.*"

Mr. Wood was certainly a key player in the decision making process, but he too, did not contact Bryan Young once. Not once did he give Mr. Young this opportunity during the suspension period. The school, therefore, has been negligent in this respect'.

Jim let this sink in.

'Thirdly. We heard from a teacher at the school that members of the school staff were advised not to make contact with Mr. Young, and that he was warned, at his suspension, not to speak to anyone at the school whilst the investigation was taking place. Yet, again, the guidelines are clear. Let me read them to you. "*Social contact with colleagues should not be precluded except where it is likely to be prejudicial to the gathering and presentation of evidence*". As no other member of staff was involved in the allegations, I cannot understand why they, the staff, and Mr.

Young, were given these warnings. The school has ignored the guidelines.'

'Fourthly, the guidelines state quite clearly in relation to disciplinary hearings like this that, "*disciplinary panel members must have regard for all the evidence presented to them*". I must remind you that I was not allowed to properly question a key witness - Mrs. Della Banks - in a way that could have exposed the reasons behind her daughter's allegations against Bryan Young. The Chairman of this panel - and without consultation with the representatives from the local authority human relations and legal departments, arbitrarily - quite arbitrarily! - decided to disallow my questions to the mother about her background. I was also prevented from asking Miss Myers about her own practice of physical contact with children. This would have highlighted the inconsistencies and inequality of treatment - and bias - against a male teacher, Bryan Young, by the management of this school.'
Jim looked at Peter Foster. 'The Chairman should have adjourned the hearing to take procedural advice from the experts who are here for this very purpose. But no! Mrs. Banks and Helen Myers were shown latitude that was unfair and, in my view, demonstrates a bias and prejudice by this Committee against Mr. Young.'

'Fifth, an overheard conversation between the Chairman of Governors, Mr. Derek Hartley, and an administrative member of the general office, has been brought to my attention, and is relevant to this appeal. Mr. Hartley was overhead by a teacher at the school discussing how the school would save money by Mr. Young's dismissal. At an industrial tribunal hearing - should it come to this - I will argue that the attitude expressed by this Governor , the *Chair* of Governors, in fact, represents overt prejudice against Mr. Young. Mr. Hartley was the chairman for the first disciplinary hearing and is an influential member of the school community. The teacher who overheard the conversation has stated that, at this stage of the process, she would prefer to remain anonymous, but she is willing to give evidence of this conversation at a tribunal, should this become necessary.'

'Sixth, the guidelines for disciplinary investigation are quite clear in that, I quote, "*the investigating officer should approach the investigation on the basis of an objective fact-finding exercise*". If it becomes necessary, I shall argue that the questions presented to the children making the allegations were often biased or leading, or that obvious follow-up questions were not asked. We must ask ourselves, why this is?'

He glanced across at Jayne Boyle. 'But whatever the reasons, the internal investigation has lacked the necessary rigour, justice, and fairness to all sides that should be implicit in this process.'

He put his notes to one side. 'For all these reasons, I put it to you that if Bryan Young's dismissal is upheld by you today, we have a strong case to take to an industrial tribunal on the grounds of unfair dismissal.' He sat down.

Chapter Twenty-six

The Committee adjourned to discuss the evidence.
Thomas told the three Governors, 'The decision must be yours; the rest of us are just here to advise, or give an opinion, if asked.'
Ali Desai was the first to speak. 'I am concerned about this issue of the industrial tribunal…'
Thomas had pushed the comments about the industrial tribunal to the back of his head, and refused to think about them. 'Ali,' he said firmly, 'Don't be…don't be influenced by those…threats! The issue is about the evidence of child abuse. This is the important issue, for me, you, the Catholic Church, your own faith - everyone with a concern for the moral welfare of children. I suggest you just focus your thoughts and discussion on the evidence presented in this case.'

Thomas's anger smouldered at the memory of Jim Osborne's assaults - on his integrity, his professionalism, his position in the school. *His* school. The headlines in the local newspaper, the excuses to parents he had had to make, and then this: these two days; the evidence against him from his own teaching staff, all done in front of the Governors and the two lackeys from the local authority; all recorded by the clerk, click, click, clicking at her computer keyboard. He looked at his deputy, sitting alone and apart, as if in a daze, and felt a swelling resentment for her part in Jim Osborne's attacks.

'I trusted her with this,' he thought. 'I trusted her to get this *right.* Yet she opens me to attacks from this…third-rater; someone who couldn't make it in the classroom; a glorified clerk from the local Union branch, not even from the regional, let alone head office.'

He thought of Bryan Young, and was conscious of himself clenching and unclenching his fists. "*A good teacher…*" Young had said of himself - echoed by Christine Evans. Christine Evans! 'I thought she was loyal,' he almost said aloud.

Her words about Young returned to flay him. "*He is a good teacher who gets good results from the children, and I just feel it's not in his nature to behave like this. His personality... probably more childlike than is good for him, particularly in a school, where that sort of...spontaneity is not exactly the norm*". Another attack on him.

'Spontaneity', he thought, 'a nice, liberal, conference word, but one that leads to disaster in a school - just like the one I inherited and had to pull back from the abyss that fool of a Head had dragged it into. Bryan Young: a *good* teacher! Oh yes! One that encourages children to be the egocentric, hedonists of the future; one that goes behind my back, his wife's back, to seduce that...'

'Head master,' said Ali Desai, 'I would like Father Kelly to be with us to help me with some issues of morality here, if that's in order? The evidence is not straight-forward. There are some troubling issues.'
'Indeed, Ali, indeed there are!'

Jim Osborne's question echoed around Jayne Boyle's head: *"What did you think of Bryan Young when he worked here? Did you like him? Did you like him? Did you like him?"*
"Did you like him?"
She thought of David. Forty years ago. David, with his easy, bantering ways.
David, who had the same black, flopping hair as Bryan Young.
David, who made her laugh. Who had mocked the nuns at her school, and the priests, and the Pope, and said anarchic things that shocked and thrilled her.
David, who had danced with her at the Mecca ballroom - that night - when she had lied to her mother about where she was going. Danced, with that easy grace Bryan Young had shown at the disco.
David, who had looked at her the way Bryan Young had looked at Della Banks.

David, who had coaxed, and soothed, and touched her, and talked, talked, talked to her. Who had talked of loving her, and wanting her, and could not stop thinking of her.
David, who had come to her house when her parents were away. And who had left her. Left her with a child in her body.
Left her, to face her parents: her father, his face grey and crumpled, in tears; her mother, her face, vicious in its rage, her eyes small and glinting; her mouth, screaming at her: "*slut, slut, slut*", striking her face with each cry of abuse.
Her mother, who had spoken to the priest and the nuns at the school. The same nuns, who had regarded her coldly, with satisfaction; the nuns who said they would pray for her soul; the nuns, who arranged for the child, her child, a daughter, to be taken, taken away from her when it was born. The daughter she would never see again.
"Did you like him?"

Father Kelly joined the group. Peter Foster said, 'Look, we need to start this off. This is how I see it. Mary Edwards - with over twenty years experience in this type of work - has recognized behaviour that she associates with the sexual grooming of children. Now, for me, the big issue is do we accept her expert judgement or not? She has read the statements and come to this conclusion, and the main issue here is, if there's a likelihood that Young has done what the girls say he did, then we have got to reject his appeal.'

Elli Curtis said, ''I think we should look closely at both the main allegations. The new evidence from Christine Evans has made me suspicious of what Latesha and Millie have said. And don't forget these girls were with Tracy Banks when she was seen drawing on the whiteboard, and challenged by Miss Boyle. They would have seen, heard and understood what was happening, and so could have just gone along with it all.

Latesha seems to have real problems, and this has made me question what she is saying. Her friend, Millie, could just be tagging along. It's a pity they were not interviewed separately. I think Millie might have been different on her own.'

She looked across at Jayne Boyle, but she seemed oblivious and emotionally detached from the discussion.

'This business of 'making it hard for him,' continued Elli, 'well, it could mean what Bryan Young said it meant - that *they* were making things hard for him, as a teacher. I can certainly imagine a teacher saying that. It's the sort of thing I might say to my own children.'

Ali Desai said, 'If this is true, I'm deeply saddened by these girls…talking about such things to each other. And they say they learned about it from a book in the school. I'm

surprised there is such a book in their class.' He glanced at Thomas, 'These are just nine year old…children!'
Thomas said, 'Ali, this is a book that Bryan Young argued for - strongly argued for. And which myself, Father Kelly, and Miss Boyle were opposed to. Wasn't that so, Father?'
Father Kelly nodded. 'But we agreed to purchase it when the majority of staff went along with his arguments.'

Elli said, 'But children see these images all around them, and I would rather they saw pictures in a book written for children, produced by a responsible publisher, than have them stumble over much worse on the Internet, or in a newsagent's shop. But we are moving away from the point here. It's about whether we believe what Latesha and Millie are saying about Bryan. As I said, I have strong doubts about the real truth of their statements.'

Peter Foster said, 'Alright, let's just park that for the moment then, and look at what Tracy Banks has said. We have stronger evidence here, I think. Why should the girl make up a story like this? This was Mary Edward's point. And there is all this business with the dancing, phone pictures on the Internet, and Bryan Young being found in the child's bedroom by the mother.'
He looked at the other two Governors. 'I don't know about you, but I was pretty disgusted by what Young had to say

about this - about why he was in the house, and his accusations against the mother. What do you make of all this?'

Elli responded. 'Yes, it was grubby stuff, on both sides. But Jim Osborne's enquiries - and what he was told by other people - the neighbour, the other parent at the disco - have cast doubt for me on Mrs. Bank's version of events.'

Peter Foster returned to the statement from the Lead Child Protection Officer. 'Mary Edwards said she felt that Young's attempts to get inside the house and be on intimate terms with the mother - was part of the pattern she described. And, whatever happened, or didn't happen between him and the mother, it presents him in a pretty sordid light, doesn't it? Doesn't it present a picture of a man who, to say the least, is a poor role model as a teacher?' He looked across at Thomas, who nodded in agreement.

Ali Desai looked at the priest. 'This aspect of what he said happened has been troubling me too… as you say, Peter, there is an issue about his morality…his character. Father Kelly, I would welcome your thoughts on this.'

The room fell silent. Thomas looked expectantly at the priest.

Father Kelly considered his reply; he was conscious of them all waiting for his verdict - *if you are the Son of God, tell this stone to become bread.*

'Of course, if we accept his version of events - and it does seem depressingly truthful in its awfulness - he should not have gone to the house with adultery in mind. You could say that he and Mrs. Banks, brought temptation upon themselves. And as Catholics we recognize temptation exists, and we say in the Lord's Prayer, "Lead us not into temptation" to guard us against sin.'

'But,' the priest continued, 'if we believe him… he did not yield to it, as Christ did not yield to it in the desert when tempted by Satan. From a Catholic perspective, God permits us to be tempted in order to test us - to see if we succumb to it. In this respect, Mr. Young did not go through with the sin of adultery; he turned away from it.' Patrick felt a weight lifting from him.

Ali leaned forward. 'My faith believes the same: that Allah, the Highest, will know our thoughts, but will judge us by our actions.'

Peter Foster said, 'Yes, yes. But he went into the child's bedroom, so what about that action, Ali? I'm not happy with the explanation he gave for that. And there is still Tracy Bank's statement about the incident in the corridor.'

Ali Desai said, 'But we have inconsistencies in this, don't we? Between what the child has said he was wearing, and what he was wearing. She says in her statement that he was wearing jeans, but he wore white slacks that day, and if she had noticed his…state of excitement, as she says, surely she would have remembered his trousers, particularly as they were so different from his normal clothing.'

'Why would she say he had kissed her and told her that he loved her?' persisted Peter Foster.

Elli raised her hand. 'We heard that Tracy was besotted with Bryan Young: saying she loved him, chasing around after him, taking his photo, and what have you. The issue for me is whether he engineered all this so he could exploit her sexually, or whether he was just the victim of this girl's obsession.'

'If we believe him, we are saying then that this girl is a liar, and that Mary Edwards has got it all wrong,' said Peter Foster.

Elli shook her head. 'Not a liar - that's too harsh. But children can fantasize about things, and it becomes real to them. My daughter has come home from school on occasions telling me things I know could not possibly have happened. But things she wants to believe can become real to her. Haven't you experience of this with children, Mr. Wood?'

Thomas said carefully, 'Your daughter is six, I believe, and much younger than Tracy Banks, who is nearly ten. We might expect that from a six or seven year old, but an older girl would be able more easily to separate fiction from reality.'

They were quiet, waiting for him to continue. 'Would you like me to give my view at this point?'

They nodded.

'I understand what you said, Father, from a faith perspective, about temptation, and resisting it. But from my perspective as a head teacher, if we are to believe him, his 'arrangement' with Mrs. Banks - whatever the outcome - was sordid and unprofessional. The school has a strict policy about contacts with families outside of school hours, and Bryan Young has shown, once again, his disregard for school policies and guidelines on teacher conduct. These are policies and guidelines you, as Governors have discussed, agreed and helped me to draft. The allegation by Tracy Banks and the other girls are serious and, although there are some inconsistencies and concerns with the specifics, the issue for me is whether the evidence presented over the past two days is strong enough to justify altering the decision reached at the first hearing. The decision will, of course, be yours.'

'It is a big responsibility for you,' continued Thomas. He smiled thinly. 'The career of a teacher is in the balance. But I am sure too, you will not forget your responsibilities to the children, our respective faiths - and the reputation of the school.'

The Governors were quiet.

Peter Moreton, from the legal department, decided it was time to speak. 'Mr. Desai, at the start of the meeting, was concerned about the possibility of this case going to industrial tribunal. He was right to be.'

Everyone turned to listen; Thomas felt the chill of dislike toward him.

'Obviously the welfare of the children is the first consideration here, and your decision must have them as your main focus. However, Mr. Osborne raised a number of issues about errors and inconsistencies in procedure that are, in my experience, likely be taken seriously by an industrial tribunal considering a case for unfair dismissal - and, if proven, could cost the school a great deal in terms of reputation - and money.'

Chapter Twenty-seven

October 11th: The Feast of St. Gummarus

Jim Osborne telephoned Bryan as soon as he heard the news. 'They have rejected the main allegations by Latesha and Millie, along with the 'inappropriate words' in the playground. They have also decided that the Tracy Banks corridor allegation should be rejected. But they still found against you for behaving unprofessionally by visiting the Banks house, and for mishandling Latesha, when you grabbed her arms.'
Bryan felt light-headed; sick with relief.

Jim continued, 'I heard unofficially from Lydia Cole that Wood still wanted you sacked for the visit to the house, but after Father Kelly's reflections on temptation and the fact that you had resisted, he couldn't really follow through with this. It's a good job you didn't fancy her when you got up close!'
'Katherine Andrews has advised the Head on an appropriate sanction - you will receive a formal written bollocking and official warning about 'your future behaviour,' and your Advanced Skills Teacher status will be reviewed. You will be reinstated at the school, subject to a period of 'supervision' for a year; I need to clarify what exactly this

involves for you. But the good news is that the pay you lost during your suspension will be returned to you. So…I'm glad for you.'

Bryan heard the sincerity in his voice and felt close to the man.
'Thanks Jim, for all your help. I would have been doomed without it, particularly the enquiries you made. But it all feels a bit of a pyrrhic victory right now.'
'Pyrrhic victory! I don't know about such things, I'm just a CDT teacher. You won; you've got your job back.' Jim had always believed and heeded the adage, 'pride cometh before a fall'. But today he didn't care; he felt good.

Bryan sat in his empty living room. "You won", Jim had said. But it didn't feel like winning. His initial feelings of relief had drained away, leaving him empty and numb. It had been ten months since the suspension. He would let Jennifer know the result, but there was no sign of a reconciliation; she was still too badly hurt and angry to consider returning to the house, and to him. The shattering of his window and daubing of his door had not been repeated, but the neighbours continued to ignore him, and did not meet his eyes or return his greetings. In recent months, he had retreated to the house. Now he would have to return to the school and face his colleagues, the children, and their parents. He would need to stay at the school and work through his period of supervision; there was no question of looking for another post elsewhere for at least a year, or longer.

**

Thomas called a staff meeting about the allegations and the result of the hearing.

'I can tell you all officially that Bryan Young will be returning to work next Monday. The Governors at the appeal hearing, having considered all the evidence were not convinced as to the reliability of some of the witness statements. They also felt that there were a number of significant procedural irregularities during the investigation.'

He looked over his glasses at Jayne Boyle; the assembled teachers followed his gaze to her, and silently tuned into the undercurrents.

Jayne sat silent; detached. She had already begun to enquire about retirement. She saw the years stretching ahead with just her mother for company.

'These irregularities would undoubtedly lead to another period of uncertainty and stress for all concerned, as Bryan Young and his Union representative would undoubtedly want to pursue this…advantage…to an industrial tribunal. The Committee decided, therefore, to find against him on an accusation of unprofessional conduct, but not the more serious charges, involving some, I must admit, disturbing allegations made by children at the school. He will, therefore, be reinstated as a teacher at this school. I have decided to move him to another class with younger children, but he will be subject to my supervision over the next twelve months.'

There was a buzz as the teachers commented on this to each other.
'What about the allegations made by the children? Do they have any substance?' asked a teacher. All the others stopped talking to listen.
'It is true to say that the statements made by the children would not stand the rigorous test of scrutiny in a criminal court, and the appeal committee decided that he should be given the benefit of the doubt - but that his behaviour should be closely supervised by me over the coming year. This I will do.'
The teachers exchanged glances with each other.

'*This I most certainly will do'* thought Thomas. 'I will also be reviewing our child protection investigation procedures in the light of the irregularities I mentioned, and I have asked Elizabeth to help me with this. Elizabeth has, as some of you know, a law degree, and has indicated her willingness to

help me with this. I'll need to adjust her teaching commitments a little to facilitate this.'
Elizabeth smiled respectfully at him, and acknowledged his comments.
More exchanged glances.
Thomas told them that, 'in her own interests,' a place for Tracy Banks had been found at another school. He said he would be calling a meeting for parents in the near future to, 'yet again,' emphasise the school policies on mobile phones, and to introduce a new behavioural contract that he would expect them all to sign. He said that discipline would be tightened, and that teachers should not hesitate to report difficult children to him.

Christine sat listening to the Head with simmering anger. She would make sure that the teachers got a more truthful account of what had happened. She had read once, and it had stuck in her mind, that the purpose of education was to turn mirrors into windows. But she had been saddened and disappointed over the years by teachers, like Thomas, who believed their purpose in life was to produce citizens who mirrored their own values and shrivelled outlook on life.
**

Bryan Young had risen early. He had not slept and had lain awake in the darkness listening to classical music on the radio until the first light came through the curtains. The house was quiet as he prepared his packed lunch; a toy lay on the floor in the corner of the room. He thought of his son, and Jennifer, and wondered if she was thinking of him today. He had dressed carefully: a dark jacket, white shirt, tie, and new flannel trousers. He had trimmed his hair.

He unlocked his bicycle and made his way to the school. It was a fine, clear day. A few parents dropping off their children at the gate looked cautiously at him. He cycled into the school playground. Thomas, from his office window, noted his arrival.

Christine had been watching for him. She came out of the school and kissed him lightly on both cheeks. He fought back his tears. She gave him a large envelope; he opened it. There was a large home-made greetings card with a drawing of him perched on his bicycle. 'Welcome back' it said, and had been signed by most of the children from his old class; Maureen O'Hara's name was at the top.

***

Published in 2011 by FeedARead Publishing

British Library C.I.P.

A CIP catalogue record for this title is available from the British Library.

Lightning Source UK Ltd.
Milton Keynes UK
UKOW050638120612

194264UK00001B/3/P